Mothers for the weekend . . .

Jessica leaned forward with excitement. "Why don't we trade places? I mean, right now? You be a kid, Mom, and Elizabeth and I will be the grown-ups. You get our projects done by Monday, we'll get your project done by Monday. In the meantime, we get to run the house. Think about it, Lizzie," she continued, turning to her twin. "We can stay up as late as we want, we get to plan our own schedules for the weekend, we can watch TV all the time and buy the food we want." She shivered with anticipation, then gave her mother a sideways glance. "But I bet she won't do it."

"Fine," Mrs. Wakefield said, crossing her arms in front of her.

Jessica couldn't believe her ears. "You mean you'll do it?"

"I just said so, didn't I?" Mrs. Wakefield told her. "If you're sure being a grown-up is so easy, this is a good weekend to try it."

SWEET VALLEY TWINS titles, published by Bantam Books. Ask your bookseller for the titles you have missed:

SWEET VALLEY TWINS

The Mother-Daughter Switch

Written by
Jamie Suzanne

Created by
FRANCINE PASCAL

BANTAM BOOKS
NEW YORK · TORONTO · LONDON · SYDNEY · AUCKLAND

THE MOTHER–DAUGHTER SWITCH
A BANTAM BOOK 0 553 40836 4

Originally published in USA by Bantam Books

First publication in Great Britain

PRINTING HISTORY
Bantam edition published 1995

The trademarks "Sweet Valley" and "Sweet Valley Twins"
are owned by Francine Pascal and are used under license by
Bantam Books and Transworld Publishers Ltd.

Conceived by Francine Pascal

Produced by Daniel Weiss Associates, Inc,
33 West 17th Street, New York, NY 10011

Bantam Books are published by Transworld Publishers Ltd,
61–63 Uxbridge Road, Ealing, London W5 5SA,
in Australia by Transworld Publishers (Australia) Pty Ltd,
15–25 Helles Avenue, Moorebank, NSW 2170,
and in New Zealand by Transworld Publishers (NZ) Ltd,
3 William Pickering Drive, Albany, Auckland.

Printed and bound in Great Britain by
Cox & Wyman Ltd, Reading, Berkshire.

To Robert Irwin Marks

One

◇

Bet I can beat that car! Jessica Wakefield told herself as a gray luxury sedan rounded the corner. It was a Thursday afternoon in early May, and Jessica was Rollerblading near her house.

A sixth-grader at Sweet Valley Middle School, Jessica was a member of the Boosters, the school cheerleading squad. On Sunday, the Boosters were having a Rollerblade-a-thon to raise money for the cancer ward of the children's hospital, and Jessica wanted to complete the course faster than anyone else.

As the driver of the car picked up speed, so did Jessica. *Faster, faster!* she said to urge herself on. All at once Jessica caught sight of the car out of the corner of her eye. It seemed to be turning right toward her! Then she realized that the car was pulling into a driveway—and that the driver probably hadn't seen her.

Jessica did the only thing possible—she flung her body onto the grassy lawn. The car pulled to a stop just a couple of feet from her head. A tall, stern-looking woman with curled gray hair lowered the driver's-side window. Jessica recognized her as one of the Wakefields' neighbors, Mrs. Wolsky.

"What on earth are you doing?" Mrs. Wolsky demanded.

Jessica struggled to her feet. She decided not to tell Mrs. Wolsky that they'd been having a race. "I—I wiped out," she replied.

Mrs. Wolsky sniffed and studied Jessica with a frown. "You're one of those Wakefield girls, aren't you?" she snapped finally.

Jessica nodded slowly.

"Humph." Mrs. Wolsky sniffed again. "If you'd gone another few feet, you could have trampled my flowers." She glared at Jessica's Rollerblades. "Those things are too dangerous for the sidewalk." Mrs. Wolsky got out of the car. "Responsibility, that's the word. Children today don't have enough of it." She looked pointedly at Jessica, then closed the car door gently. "Responsibility," she said again. "By the way, are you all right?"

Jessica's knee hurt like anything, but she wasn't about to let Mrs. Wolsky know. "I'm fine," she said. "Thank you."

Mrs. Wolsky sniffed once more. "I work very hard on those flowers," she continued. "It would be very disappointing if anything happened to them. Responsibility, now." She eyed Jessica one last time and disappeared into her house.

Jessica slowly skated toward home. Her body ached all over. *What is Mrs. Wolsky talking about?* she said to herself angrily. *I'm a totally responsible person. I don't go around destroying people's flowers. Besides, she should pay more attention to where she turns her car.*

Jessica sat down on the front steps of the Wakefield house and began to loosen her Roller-blades. The screen door banged shut as Steven, Jessica's fourteen-year-old brother, came out holding his new video camera. "Hey, what happened?" Steven said cheerfully. "Fall down a hole?"

"Steven, get out of here!" Jessica snapped. "I almost got run over by a car. And it was the driver's fault, not mine." *Well, mostly,* she added to herself.

"Seriously?" Steven asked, smiling. "Hey, mind if I take your picture? This'd be a great shot in a movie I'm going to make: *The Sad Truth About Accident Victims.* Yup," he said as he stuck the video camera in Jessica's face, "some victims of accidents have their beauty messed up, but others were just born looking that way. . . ."

"Steven Wakefield!" Jessica shouted in protest. "Get that thing away from me!"

". . . like this one," Steven continued, panning the camera across Jessica's sweaty forehead and down to her banged-up knees. Then he raised an eyebrow at her. "I thought you wanted to be in the movies."

"Not this kind of movie I don't!" Jessica snapped. "I'm going to be in something real, where I get to wear a glamorous costume and plenty of makeup. And it'll have a real director, not some toad of a brother who thinks he's going to be famous."

"Well, you'll need a *lot* of makeup," Steven said, pointing the camera again at Jessica's face.

"Stop the film or I'll break your camera," Jessica threatened him. "I mean it."

Steven snorted, but he stopped filming and sat down beside Jessica. "What you don't realize," he said, "is that you're looking at the next Steven Starholtz." He sat back proudly and folded his arms.

Jessica laughed loudly. "You?" Steven Starholtz's movies were terrific: the dangerous lion stalking the parks of Los Angeles, the cute cuddly cave creature who befriended a little girl. "Well, call me when you make a billion dollars."

"No, seriously," Steven protested. "Haven't you noticed that we have the same first name? If he can do it, so can I."

"Yeah, right," Jessica said, wincing as she moved her leg a little too quickly.

The screen door banged again, and Jessica's twin sister, Elizabeth, walked out. "There you are, Jess! I've just figured it out."

"What did you figure out?" Jessica asked, sliding over to make room for her twin.

"My media-class project," explained Elizabeth.

"I have to tape three shows and review them, and I've chosen the three I want to do." She patted the *TV Guide* in her lap.

"There's no school tomorrow," Jessica pointed out. "It's conference day for the teachers. When's this thing due, anyway?"

"Monday," Elizabeth told her.

"And you're working on it now?" Jessica asked, her eyes widening.

Jessica was always amazed at how much time her sister spent on her schoolwork. On the outside, the girls looked exactly alike. Both had long blond hair and sparkling bluish-green eyes. When they smiled, each girl showed a dimple in her left cheek. But on the inside, they were as different as could be.

Jessica lived for her friends. She was a member of the Unicorn Club, an exclusive group made up of the prettiest and most popular girls at Sweet Valley Middle School. She loved to talk about boys, clothes, and soap operas.

Elizabeth, on the other hand, was quiet and thoughtful. While she always made time for family and friends, most of her energy went into reading and working on the sixth-grade newspaper, which she edited. But despite their differences, the two sisters were the best of friends.

"I want to get just the right shows," Elizabeth explained, opening the magazine. "I'm going to start tomorrow night with *Mrs. Mary Butterworth*."

"No offense or anything, but that's a really boring

show," Jessica said. "Why don't you just take my *Days of Turmoil* tape?" *Days of Turmoil* was Jessica's favorite soap opera.

"I think *Mrs. Mary Butterworth* is a great show," Elizabeth argued.

Jessica looked at Steven and grimaced.

"I've got an idea," Steven said. "Why don't I make you a movie? You can be the first to review a great Steven Wakefield film."

"Don't listen to him, Lizzie," Jessica advised. "He thinks he's the next Steven Starholtz."

"Seriously? You?" Elizabeth stared at her brother, a grin playing around the corners of her lips.

Steven picked up the camera menacingly and aimed it at the girls. "Let me tell you something about Steven Starholtz," he said. "He killed his sisters."

"He what?" Elizabeth said, wrinkling her forehead in alarm.

"In a movie," Steven added. "He made horror films when he was my age, and his sisters were the stars. They would scream like crazy, and there was blood everywhere." He grinned at them.

"Really?" Jessica asked. "Hey, maybe we could—"

"Jessica!" Elizabeth turned to her twin. "You wouldn't—oh, Jess, what happened?" She gasped as she noticed Jessica's scratches.

Jessica told her the whole story. To make it a little more dramatic, she added that Mrs. Wolsky swerved around the corner without signaling her turn.

"Good thing I was wearing a helmet," she finished. "I think maybe I'll go lie down for a little while, though."

"What, and miss the party?" Steven said.

"The party?" both girls exclaimed together.

Steven shrugged. "Aren't you having a party tonight? That mother-daughter thing?"

Jessica and Elizabeth stared at each other in horror. "The Mother's Day picnic," Jessica said slowly. "I forgot all about it."

"Me, too," Elizabeth whispered. "Mom is going to kill us."

It was all coming back to Jessica. In honor of Mother's Day on Sunday and the long weekend from school, the twins had invited their friends to a mother-daughter barbecue at their house late Thursday afternoon.

Jessica checked her watch. "We have twenty minutes," she announced. "We're probably dead meat."

"I feel terrible," Elizabeth said a few minutes later, lugging a lawn chair across the backyard.

Her twin looked up from the picnic table, which she was hastily washing off. "Well, it's not really our fault," she said, scowling. "It's not like we had lots of time, if you know what I mean."

Elizabeth sighed. "I just hate to let Mom down, that's all. What were we supposed to get, anyway?"

"Napkins," Jessica said. She pointed a finger at

Elizabeth. "You were supposed to get napkins and ketchup and potato chips, too."

"No," Elizabeth said, trying to think back to the night when they'd planned the party. "You were supposed to get the chips." She set the chair down in a corner of the yard.

"No, I wasn't!" Jessica shot back, dropping the sponge and whirling to face Elizabeth. "I was right there. Mom definitely told you to get the chips."

"No, she didn't, Jess!" Elizabeth argued. "It was you—" Abruptly, she stopped. "Did you get anything at all?"

"No," Jessica admitted in a small voice. "Did you?"

Elizabeth shook her head. *All I remembered was to send out the invitations,* she said to herself. *And it looks like that was a big mistake.*

"Well," Jessica offered, "it's not the end of the world. Mom will just have to understand that we sort of spaced the whole thing. I've been very busy, you know, getting sponsors for the Rollerblade-a-thon. Can you believe I'm up to seventy-five dollars already?"

Elizabeth looked at her sister wearily.

"And you've been busy on that class project," Jessica pointed out. "Where were we supposed to get the time to do those errands? Mom is just going to have to take care of it. That's what moms are for, right?"

Elizabeth furrowed her brow. "I don't know,

Jessica. I don't think we've been too responsible."

"Mom's probably at the supermarket right now, getting the drinks and stuff," Jessica said confidently.

"Was she supposed to get the drinks?" Elizabeth asked. "I thought you were supposed to get the drinks."

"Relax, Lizzie," Jessica said, picking the sponge back up. "Mom'll come through. She always does."

"I hope you're right." Elizabeth sighed. "But I'm not so sure. Mom's awfully busy these days."

"She is?" Jessica set the sponge down again.

Elizabeth felt a wave of irritation. *Quit stopping all the time, Jess,* she thought. "Mom said she really needed us to cooperate," she reminded her twin. "Remember? She said she was way behind on a decorating project for Mrs. Wolsky—you know, the woman you almost ran into. Mrs. Wolsky is making things hard for Mom, so Mom asked us to get some things for the party. She said she couldn't do everything by herself."

"Well," Jessica said assuredly, "it'll come out OK in the end."

"I hope so," Elizabeth said, looking at the half-sponged table.

Five minutes later, Jessica heard her mother's car pull into the driveway. "Come on, Lizzie," she said, grabbing her sister by the arm. "Mom's here. Don't forget to smile!"

As Mrs. Wakefield began to walk toward the house, the girls came out, grinning broadly.

"Hello, Mom," Jessica sang out.

"Yes, hi, Mom," Elizabeth chimed in.

"Hi, girls," Mrs. Wakefield said, smiling back. She gave them each a hug. "Did you have a good day at school?"

"Just fine, thanks," Jessica said. "You look tired." She patted her mother's hand.

"I certainly feel tired," her mother replied, laughing. "It's been quite a day."

"I can imagine!" Jessica said. "All that shopping and everything really takes a lot out of you."

Mrs. Wakefield looked puzzled. But before she had a chance to speak, Elizabeth piped up. "Is Mrs. Wolsky giving you a hard time?" she asked sympathetically.

"You could say that," Mrs. Wakefield agreed, putting an arm around each girl's shoulder. "I never know why you girls are in such a hurry to grow up. Being an adult is terribly hard work."

"Yeah, well, shall we help you unload?" Jessica asked.

"Help me unload what?" Mrs. Wakefield frowned. "I suppose you could help me unload myself. Maybe you'd like to pick me up and carry me inside—you know, the way I used to carry you when you were little. Goodness knows I'm tired enough."

Jessica caught Elizabeth's anxious glance.

"Can you imagine," Mrs. Wakefield continued, shaking her head and smiling, "I drove all the way home from the furniture store on about two teaspoonfuls of gas. I just couldn't put up with refilling the tank. I hope the car will start tomorrow. In fact, if you don't mind, I think I'll go lie down for a little while."

"But—" Jessica gulped. This didn't sound good at all. "We came out to help you unload all the stuff for the party. The things you were supposed to buy. You know, the ice—"

"And the napkins," Elizabeth put in.

"You didn't forget, did you?" Jessica opened her eyes wide and stared imploringly at her mother.

Mrs. Wakefield was staring back. Then she gasped. "It's Thursday, isn't it? The mother-daughter party. And I forgot all about it." She looked from one girl to the other. "I've just been so busy lately," she explained. "I'm so sorry."

"Oh, that's all right," Elizabeth said, looking a little uncomfortable.

Jessica shot her sister a dirty look. What did she mean, "That's all right"? "But the guests arrive in less than ten minutes," she began, "and—" She paused.

"What's the problem?" Mrs. Wakefield looked questioningly at Jessica. "So we're missing the napkins and a couple of other small things," she said in a cheerful tone as she walked into the kitchen. "We had the hamburger patties in the freezer this morning, and you girls picked up charcoal, drinks, and ketchup, right?"

"Actually, we didn't get the charcoal," Jessica said, deciding to stick up for herself as she followed her mother into the kitchen.

Mrs. Wakefield was reaching to open the freezer. She stopped and turned to face the girls. "You didn't get the charcoal?"

"We weren't supposed to buy the charcoal," Jessica said quickly. "You were supposed to buy the charcoal."

Mrs. Wakefield looked confused. "No," she said slowly, "I remember asking one of you to buy the charcoal. I'm almost positive."

"And you were supposed to buy the ketchup and the drinks, too," Jessica added, trying to cover her embarrassment.

"I wasn't supposed to buy the ketchup and the drinks," Mrs. Wakefield said, a little more sharply. "If you didn't buy ketchup and drinks and charcoal, what *did* you buy?"

There was a moment's pause while Mrs. Wakefield looked from one twin to the other.

Elizabeth looked down at her hands.

"You forgot the whole thing?" Mrs. Wakefield surmised, tightening her mouth.

Jessica slowly nodded her head.

"Listen, girls, I really don't need this after the kind of week I've had," Mrs. Wakefield said. "I thought you were old enough to handle this."

"Couldn't you quickly drive to the store?"

Jessica asked hopefully. "At least we could get the charcoal and a few bottles of pop."

"If you knew how busy I've been," Mrs. Wakefield said grimly, "you wouldn't ask me to do a thing. Aside from which, I couldn't possibly drive to the store and back on two teaspoonfuls of gas." She checked her watch. "With the lines the way they are at the gas station and the supermarket, I'd be lucky to get back here before the party ends."

"We're sorry," Elizabeth said humbly.

"Why don't we call someone who's coming and ask them to help us out, quick?" Jessica asked. "Maybe Mandy or someone has a bag of charcoal they could bring."

The doorbell rang. "Too late," Mrs. Wakefield said, throwing up her hands. "Oh, boy, is this ever going to be fun!"

"Hey, do that again, Mom!" came a voice from the hall. With a start, Jessica looked up and saw Steven, his video camera trained directly on Mrs. Wakefield.

"Answer the door, Jessica," Mrs. Wakefield directed. "And as for you, Steven Wakefield," she said icily, "if you don't point that thing away from me this minute, I'll break it into a thousand tiny pieces."

Two

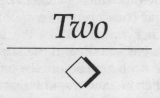

"This lemonade tastes pretty weak, Jessica." Ellen Riteman, a member of the Unicorn Club, joined Jessica on the patio. "Don't you have some pop?"

Jessica dragged her thoughts away from Lila and Janet. "The lemonade is weak?" she asked, putting on an exaggerated look of surprise. "Gee, that's funny."

"Here, taste it," Ellen offered, thrusting the glass toward Jessica.

"Um, no, that's OK," Jessica said, backing up. She decided to take Ellen's word for it. She'd found only one package of lemonade mix in the entire house. In order to make the drinks stretch a little further, she had mixed the lemonade powder with three pitchers of water, not the one pitcher the directions called for. But Jessica wasn't about to explain that to Ellen. "I'm so sorry," she said, taking the glass. "Here, let me fix it for you."

"Thanks. And if you could add more ice, I'd appreciate it," Ellen said.

More ice? Jessica thought. She hoped there *was* more ice.

"Sheesh, there's *nothing* in this house," Jessica said, opening drawers in the refrigerator. She had just given Ellen a new cup of watery lemonade with extra sugar and had decided it would be a good idea to hang out in the kitchen for a while. "Not even a few lousy olives. Oh, hey—there's this." She pulled out a piece of wax paper with six pickle slices inside it.

"*Great,*" Elizabeth said with emphasis, looking up from a package of bologna she was unwrapping. Bologna was all there was for dinner, and Steven, who might have been able to ride his bike to the grocery store to pick up something else, was nowhere to be found.

Jessica sighed and opened the big drawer at the bottom. She stared. It was full to the brim with tomatoes.

"Well, we have tomatoes," she said. "*Tons* of them. We'll cut up a bunch and people can put tomatoes in their sandwiches."

"That's funny," Elizabeth said, leaning over Jessica's shoulder. "I wonder where they came from?"

"Who cares?" Jessica said, passing a couple to Elizabeth. "Let's cut them up quick and get them out there to Mom."

"I hope people like tomatoes," Elizabeth said, as Jessica grabbed one after the other.

"Of course people like tomatoes," Jessica said loudly. "Everybody'll love tomato-and-bologna sandwiches. With plenty of mustard. I mean, don't you like tomatoes?"

"Well, yes," Elizabeth agreed, still staring at the drawer, "but I'm not sure I like tomatoes all that much."

The twins silently cut four tomatoes into thin slices. Loading them onto another china plate, Jessica sighed. "This would be so much easier if Mom had just done her shopping."

"Well—" Elizabeth began doubtfully.

"I mean it, Lizzie!" Jessica interrupted. "We'd have burgers and chips instead of stale pretzels and watery lemonade, and everybody would be having a good time, and we wouldn't be serving our friends tomato sandwiches!"

Elizabeth smiled mischievously. "I thought you said everyone liked tomato sandwiches."

"Well, I lied!" Jessica burst out. "This party's horrible. I'm ruined! How can I show my face at school on Monday? Or at the Rollerblade-a-thon? And the worst thing is, it isn't even my fault!"

Elizabeth was about to say something, but she shut her mouth instead.

"I'm serious!" Jessica said. "I refuse to go out there any more tonight. Every single time I do, someone's complaining, or laughing at me, and I'm sick of it. So now it's your turn. I'll do all the inside stuff, and you go mix with the guests. All right?" Not waiting for an answer, Jessica thrust the plate of tomatoes into Elizabeth's hands.

"What inside stuff?" Elizabeth wanted to know. "Everything's done."

"I'll just stay here and wait for the ice to freeze!" Jessica yelled. As Elizabeth headed out the door, Jessica tossed the pickle slices onto the tomato plate. "And take these!" she added. "If you cut them into quarters, everyone might get a pickle, too!"

"What's on that plate, Elizabeth?" Janet asked eagerly as Elizabeth hurried by.

Elizabeth smiled as brightly as she could. "Tomatoes!" she said, hoping her enthusiasm would be catching.

"Oh." Janet's face fell. "I thought maybe it was hamburgers."

"I'm allergic to tomatoes," Lila added, turning up her nose.

Allergic? Elizabeth thought. "But you eat pizza," she pointed out.

"Well, I'm only allergic to regular tomatoes," Lila explained. "I'm not allergic to tomatoes when they're in tomato sauce."

"A lot of people are like that," Janet assured

Elizabeth. "I'd say over half the Unicorns only can eat tomatoes in sauce. Maybe even more than that. Don't you think so, Lila?"

Lila nodded in agreement.

Janet fixed Elizabeth with a look. "Actually, Jessica might be the one exception to the rule. She likes tomatoes, doesn't she?"

"I think she doesn't like them as much as she used to," Elizabeth answered honestly. She dashed over to the picnic table and set down the plate. Mandy Miller was looking over the bologna platter with a frown.

"Oh, are those hamburgers?" she said with interest.

Elizabeth wondered if she should put a sign on the plate that said NO, THESE ARE NOT HAMBURGERS, BUT THEY'RE BETTER THAN YOU PROBABLY THINK. She smiled widely again. "We thought we'd try some nice fresh tomatoes instead."

"Fresh?" Mandy stared at the plate. "Those don't look too fresh to me."

"Oh, believe me, they're delicious." Elizabeth picked up a slice and put it in her mouth. "Mmm. So tasty," she said, wishing she were a more convincing actress. "I eat bologna and tomato sandwiches whenever I can."

"Really?" Mandy looked at Elizabeth curiously.

Elizabeth felt herself beginning to turn red. "Well, whenever we have bologna and tomatoes in the house," she corrected herself. "Which isn't all that often, I guess. Mostly when we have company."

"Oh." Mandy nodded. "So you only buy bologna and tomatoes to serve to your guests?"

"Right," Elizabeth replied, wondering how to change the subject. "You wouldn't want to eat it every day, you know."

"Well, I know I wouldn't," Mandy agreed, shaking her head vigorously.

"So let me make you a big sandwich!" Elizabeth picked up a slice of bread and held it out to Mandy.

"No, thanks." Mandy curled her lip. "I don't like bologna all that much."

"Oh. Well, how about a plain tomato sandwich?" Elizabeth tried.

Mandy shook her head. "I don't like tomatoes all that much either. But thanks anyway. I guess."

As Mandy strolled off, Elizabeth felt her heart sink. Normally, she tried to look on the bright side of things, but she had to admit it: this party was not a success.

"I'm *not* going out there," Jessica said as Elizabeth came back into the kitchen.

"Yes, you are," Elizabeth said, checking one of the ice trays. "The ice is ready, and there's absolutely nothing more for you to do in here." She cracked the ice into the bucket and clutched her sister's arm.

"I'm not moving and that's final." She yanked her arm away from Elizabeth's hold.

Elizabeth was considering dragging Jessica out from the kitchen, when suddenly there was a commotion on the patio. Janet Howell, an eighth grader and the president of the Unicorn Club, Rollerbladed into the house and came to a perfect stop just in front of the twins. She was followed by several other Unicorns. Ellen Riteman and Lila Fowler looked as though they were trying hard to hold back giggles. "We're leaving now," Janet said. "But we wanted to ask you something first."

"What's that?" Elizabeth asked.

"We were wondering why you didn't have a regular barbecue," Ellen asked.

"Oh." Elizabeth felt her cheeks heating up. She looked at Jessica for help.

Jessica looked steadfastly at the ground.

"Well," Elizabeth continued, "we just thought we'd do something different for a change!" She smiled and gestured with her arms to show what a great idea she thought it was.

Janet and Lila looked at each other with a smirk. Ellen snickered.

"I see." Janet smiled at the twins. "It was different, all right. Congratulations. Jessica, we'll see *you* on Sunday." She turned to go and then stopped. "And by the way, you have to tell me the name of the store where you got that wonderful lemonade. Or should I call it 'water ade'?"

Jessica looked as if she wanted to crawl into a hole. As for Elizabeth, she hadn't thought it was possible to turn any redder. But as the other girls broke into laughter, she discovered she was wrong.

Three

"Well, I hope you'll come back soon," Mrs. Wakefield said half an hour later, forcing a grin. It was just as well that Amy Sutton and her mother were the only guests still around. She didn't think she could smile much longer.

"Oh, we will," Mrs. Sutton replied with a cough.

"Can we help clean up?" Amy asked.

"No, no, the girls and I will take care of it," Mrs. Wakefield said hastily. *After I take care of those girls,* she said to herself. "Thanks very much anyway, Amy."

"All right. Bye."

"Good night!" Mrs. Wakefield stood in the doorway, smiling her widest, until Mrs. Sutton was out of sight. Then she hurried off to the patio.

* * *

Jessica sat quietly at the picnic table, staring off into space and hoping her mother wouldn't bother to come out back. Next to her, Elizabeth sat wiping the table, very slowly, with a sponge.

Mrs. Wakefield walked into the yard and settled comfortably into a lawn chair. Jessica squirmed. "So!" Mrs. Wakefield said. "Did you girls have a good time?"

Elizabeth shook her head.

"You *know* we didn't, Mom," Jessica put in. "I probably won't be able to set foot in school after today. My friends probably will never speak to me again."

"No?" Mrs. Wakefield asked, her eyes narrowing. "Suppose I tell you whose fault it is. Well, I thought I could count on a little help from my two sixth-grade daughters. I didn't think I'd have to plan every last detail of this party myself. I have far too much work for that!" With each sentence, her voice grew louder and angrier. "I can't tell you how upset and disappointed I am. Jessica, I'm sorry if you've ruined your social life for good, but, young lady, you've got no one to blame but yourself."

"But that's not fair!" Jessica protested.

"What do you mean, fair?" Mrs. Wakefield asked coldly. "Did you remember to get the charcoal? No! The napkins? No! How about the ketchup, or the drinks, or the chips? Was that 'fair'?"

"Well, but I wasn't the only one," Jessica argued. She wasn't about to let this attack pass without defending herself. "I wasn't the only one who forgot to pick stuff up. I wasn't even supposed to get the chips or the charcoal. That was Elizabeth's job!"

"I don't care whose job it was," Mrs. Wakefield said.

"Well, you're not the only one who's busy, you know. This Booster project takes up all my time. Why aren't you picking on Elizabeth instead? She hasn't had hardly anything to do."

"Jess!" Elizabeth burst out.

"Well, it's true, Elizabeth," Jessica went on, not quite daring to look her sister in the eye. "I mean, all *you've* got to do is your stupid media project. You could've just borrowed my *Days of Turmoil* tape. It takes about five minutes to review the whole thing. Then you would have had plenty of time to go to the store and pick up all the things I couldn't because *I didn't have time!*"

"*Children!*" Mrs. Wakefield's voice boomed out over theirs.

The girls stopped bickering.

"This argument is pointless," Mrs. Wakefield told them. "I don't care who's busier than who. What matters is that both of you let me down. And yourselves down, too," she added. "There's no excuse for that. None. Do I make myself clear?"

"Yes, Mom," Jessica grumbled, wishing she were somewhere else.

Elizabeth nodded. "We're sorry," she said.

"I'm sure you are," Mrs. Wakefield said more

gently. She sat back and crossed her legs. "There's one more thing I'd like to say. I hear you two talking about how busy you are, but I don't think you really know what 'busy' means. Homework and Rollerblading are a breeze compared to what I go through every day."

The twins exchanged looks.

"Your father and I have to do our work, whether we like it or not," Mrs. Wakefield continued. "And sometimes it seems that the toughest part of our work is being parents to a couple of irresponsible kids!" she folded her arms and glanced crossly from one twin to the other. "You two are incredibly lucky to be young."

Jessica felt her cheeks get hot. "That's not true!" she shot back. "Being a kid is hard work. Being a mom is what's easy."

Mrs. Wakefield gave a bitter laugh. "Don't be silly, Jessica."

"I'm serious!" Jessica insisted. "You never listen to me, do you? I always have to listen to you, but you never listen to me. That's one reason why it's so tough to be a kid."

"Jessica—" Mrs. Wakefield began.

"Jessica's right, Mom," Elizabeth cut in. "Think about it. You can always turn down Mrs. Wolsky's decorating job if you want to, but I can't just skip my homework."

"Face it, Mom," Jessica continued. "Your life is a piece of cake. You don't worry about boys. You're not afraid that your friends are whispering mean things about you. You don't have to think about wearing the right clothes, or sitting next to the right people in homeroom. It's so *easy* to be a mom."

Mrs. Wakefield just shook her head. "You have absolutely no idea," she said heatedly. "Remember, I was a kid once, but you girls have never been moms."

"Yeah, well, you were a kid back in the Dark Ages!" Jessica exclaimed.

Elizabeth nodded. "Things are really different today, Mom. You wouldn't believe how much homework they assign us these days."

"And think of all the new stuff that's been discovered since you were twelve. Microwave ovens and personal computers—" Jessica emphasized each word by leaning forward and ticking it off on her fingers.

"VCRs," Elizabeth put in, using the same tone of voice.

A ghost of a smile flickered on Mrs. Wakefield's lips. "First of all, girls, I had lots more homework back in the 'Dark Ages' than you think. Second, machines like VCRs and microwaves are supposed to make life easier, not harder." Imitating Jessica, she ticked off the reasons on her fingers one by one. "But you'll just have to wait until you're grown up to see the truth of what I'm saying. Once again, I want you to know I'm very, very disappointed in you."

You'll just have to wait . . . An idea was struggling to get out of Jessica's mind.

Standing up, Mrs. Wakefield looked at the remains of the party and shook her head. "I guess we'd better get this disaster cleaned up."

"But we don't!" Jessica blurted out, the idea taking shape.

Mrs. Wakefield's head snapped up. "What's that?"

"I mean we don't have to wait till we're adults," Jessica explained quickly, leaning forward with excitement. "Why don't we trade places? I mean, right now? You be the kid, Mom, and Elizabeth and I will be the grown-ups."

"For how long?" Mrs. Wakefield asked sourly.

"For the weekend," Jessica explained, thinking hard. "Till Monday morning. You can do the Rollerblading for me, since you say it's so easy."

"And my media-class project," Elizabeth added, her face lighting up, too.

"We'd be in charge of all the things you're usually in charge of. Planning the meals—" Jessica tried to think of something else that Mrs. Wakefield was in charge of. Just then it was hard to think of anything.

"Bossing Steven around," Elizabeth suggested with a smile.

"Right, bossing Steven around," Jessica said with delight. "And we'll do that decorating job for Mrs. Wolsky, too. It can't be that difficult."

"Oh, is that right?" Mrs. Wakefield asked with interest. Now she was smiling.

"No possible way," Jessica assured her. "You get our projects done by Monday, we'll get your project done by Monday. In the meantime, we get to run the house. Think about it, Lizzie," she continued, turning to her twin. "We can stay up as late as we want, we get to plan our own schedules for the weekend, we can watch TV all the time and buy the food we want." She shivered with anticipation, then gave her mother a sideways glance. "But I bet she won't do it."

"Fine," Mrs. Wakefield said, crossing her arms in front of her.

Jessica couldn't believe her ears. "You mean you'll do it?"

"I just said so, didn't I?" Mrs. Wakefield told her. "If you're sure being a grown-up is so easy, this is a good weekend to try it."

"Now, Elizabeth, your media-class project," Mrs. Wakefield said a few moments later. Elizabeth was leaning excitedly forward as she, Jessica, and Mrs. Wakefield laid out the ground rules of the mother-daughter switch. "What's it all about?"

"Well," Elizabeth explained, "you tape three TV shows and write a review of them."

"That's it?"

Elizabeth stared at her mother. "What do you mean?" she asked suspiciously.

"In my day we had to take tests and write research papers," Mrs. Wakefield said, running her hand through her hair. "What a breeze! I can't be-lieve you kids ever complain about your work-load."

Elizabeth decided to ignore that comment. "I al-ready chose the three shows," she went on. "They're—"

"They're really boring," Jessica muttered.

"Just a minute!" Mrs. Wakefield held up her hand. "Since it's *my* project, *I* get to choose the shows *I* want to tape—am I right?"

Elizabeth hesitated. "I guess so," she said un-comfortably. She realized how much she had been looking forward to reviewing the next episode of *Mrs. Mary Butterworth*. "What kinds of shows do you think you'll pick?" she asked.

"Oh, I don't know yet," Mrs. Wakefield said lightly. "I may not pick anything till nine o'clock Sunday night. Who knows? Gosh, we've only just started, and already I'm having loads of fun being a kid!"

"But you *will* do a good job on my project, won't you?" Elizabeth began, looking over at her sister for help.

"Oh, sure, Elizabeth," Mrs. Wakefield said soothingly. "No problem at all. 'Piece of cake,' as I think someone said a few minutes ago. Now, Jessica. What's your incredibly important assign-ment all about?"

Jessica frowned. "It *is* incredibly important. And you really have to do it right, Mom."

"Do it right?" Mrs. Wakefield snapped. "Of course I'll do it right. What do you think I am—irresponsible or something?"

Elizabeth winced.

"It's for the cancer ward of the children's hospital," Jessica explained. "First you have to get some more pledges. I got about seventy-five dollars, but I know Lila and Janet will have hundreds and hundreds of dollars each."

"Pledges? No sweat," Mrs. Wakefield said. "And then you Rollerblade how far on Sunday?"

"It's a three-mile loop," Jessica said. Elizabeth thought she could see a flash of concern cross her sister's face. "Listen, Mom, are you sure you can do this? We can cancel the switch if you want."

"What, just because I've never been on Rollerblades before?" their mother replied. "All kids can Rollerblade. Now that I'm a kid, it'll be easy."

"And in exchange for that, all you have to do is decorate Mrs. Wolsky's sunporch," Mrs. Wakefield finished.

"Oh, it's just the sunporch?" Elizabeth exclaimed, relieved. *That should make it easier.*

"Just the sunporch," Mrs. Wakefield repeated, flashing them a cat-that-ate-the-canary grin.

Elizabeth studied her mother's face. "So tell us more about this job. What's going to make it so hard?"

"Hard?" Mrs. Wakefield said with mock horror. "Who said anything about hard? Adults' jobs are easy, remember. Decorating one little sunporch should be a snap." She snapped her fingers and grinned again.

Elizabeth looked at Jessica with alarm.

Jessica ignored her sister's look. "Sounds good to me," she said firmly. "And we get to boss Steven around as much as we want?"

"Well, you can't put him in any kind of danger," Mrs. Wakefield explained. "But I'm sure you can have lots of fun with him all the same."

Elizabeth smiled. She liked the idea of telling Steven what to do.

"So!" Mrs. Wakefield said brightly. "How about if we start right now? Let's see." She sat down and checked her watch. "Your father is due home any minute. I'll bet he'd like to be a kid, too. Don't you think? We'll go for a walk in the park."

"But the cleanup?" Elizabeth protested, motioning around the yard and patio.

"Oh, the *cleanup*," Mrs. Wakefield said as though she were noticing the mess for the first time. She put her hand on her chin, a thoughtful expression on her face. Then she shrugged and stood up. "It'll just have to wait," she said cheerfully.

"Can't your *walk* wait?" Elizabeth asked.

"Oh, no," Mrs. Wakefield said, shaking her head vigorously. "You only think so because you're an adult. If you were a kid, you'd understand that it has to be done *right now*."

Elizabeth wrinkled her brow. What her mother

was saying sounded vaguely familiar. "Mom, are you trying to tease us?"

"*Me?*" Mrs. Wakefield said with a grin. "I don't think so. You have to remember that I haven't been a kid for a long time. Luckily, I've been taking lessons for quite a few years. From a couple of experts." She turned to the patio door. "There's Dad's car. I'm off!"

"But that's not fair!" Jessica called after her.

"Hey, would you mind moving inside? We're losing the light out here." The twins whirled around. Steven was crouched in the fork of Elizabeth's favorite tree at the back of the yard. His movie camera was pointed right at them.

"Have you been filming us the whole time?" Elizabeth demanded.

Steven chuckled.

"Mo-om!" Jessica shouted. "Make him stop!"

"Mom?" Mrs. Wakefield asked innocently. "Mom who?"

Four

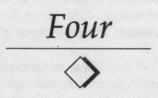

"*First* we have him wash the windows," Jessica said to Elizabeth later that evening. The twins were sitting at the dining room table. In front of them was a sheet with the title "CHORES FOR STEVEN WAKEFIELD" written in bright-red Magic Marker. "When he's done with that, we'll send him to the grocery store."

A slow smile lit up Elizabeth's face. "Jessica, you're a genius!"

"I know," Jessica said modestly. "Face it, Elizabeth. We're golden. This mother-daughter switch is terrific. We'll make Mom and Dad and Steven do all the cleaning up. We'll only cook foods that we like."

"We can go to bed late," Elizabeth added.

"And what are the drawbacks?" Jessica asked. "Decorate one silly little sunporch. That's it! This is going to be *sooo* great."

Just then, the telephone rang.

"I'll get it," Jessica said. She sprinted to the living room extension next door. "Hello?" she blurted into the receiver. Then, remembering she was now a grown-up, she lowered her voice and tried again. "I mean—Wakefield residence."

"Mrs. Wakefield, please," came a curiously familiar voice.

"I'm sorry, she's not in just now," Jessica said, pronouncing each word very carefully.

A sniff came from the other end of the line. "When do you expect her back?"

"Oh, I couldn't say just now," Jessica said. She found she could keep her tone of voice by sticking her nose in the air. "Perhaps I could take a message?"

Sniff. "Who is this?" the woman demanded.

"Who is *this*?" Jessica countered.

"This is Mrs. Wolsky, down the street," Mrs. Wolsky said loudly, "and I want to know why Mrs. Wakefield isn't doing anything about my sunporch."

Mrs. Wolsky! Jessica thought. No wonder the voice sounded familiar. "Ah, Mrs. Wolsky," Jessica said, playing for time. "Hasn't she told you that she's got it *perfectly* under control?"

"No, she hasn't," Mrs. Wolsky snapped. "She promised to show me her latest design this evening, but I haven't seen it. And we're on a very tight schedule. A *very* tight schedule."

"I'm sure you are," Jessica agreed. She didn't like the way this conversation was going. Elizabeth came to the doorway, a questioning look on her face. "But not to worry. She's getting help from an excellent team of decorators. She'll have it ready for you whenever you say."

"Well, she'd better." Sniff, sniff.

"I'm sure she will, Mrs. Wolsky," Jessica said. "My mother is a very responsible person."

"Hmm." Apparently Mrs. Wolsky wasn't convinced. "Your mother, hey? Are you that little girl who nearly destroyed my flowers this afternoon?"

"No, no, that wasn't me," Jessica lied, crossing her fingers. "That must have been my sister." She glanced away as Elizabeth raised her eyebrows at her. "I was somewhere else at the time the—um—accident took place."

Sniff. Then a sigh. "Well, I think I'll not leave a message. Is anyone responsible at your house just now?"

"There's me," Jessica said hotly.

Sniff.

"I'm responsible, Mrs. Wolsky, really I am," Jessica said.

"Your sister wasn't this afternoon," Mrs. Wolsky pointed out tartly.

"Well, I'm not my sister," Jessica said truthfully. Her voice was beginning to sound normal again, so she stuck her nose back in the air. "What do you need, Mrs. Wolsky? Whatever I can do for you, just let me know."

"Hmm. Very well. I shall drop off a key to my house. Please tell your mother I shall trust her, though perhaps against my better judgment. I leave town early tomorrow, and I'll be away for the entire weekend. You're quite sure you can get the key to your mother?"

"Quite sure," Jessica agreed, rolling her eyes and pretending to salute. Watching from the doorway, Elizabeth giggled.

Sniff. "Very well." Click. Jessica stood looking at the phone in her hand.

"So what was that all about?" Elizabeth asked.

"Oh, nothing," Jessica assured her. "Just Mrs. Wolsky looking for Mom. She's going to drop a key here in a few minutes, that's all."

"It didn't *sound* like that was all," Elizabeth said.

Jessica gave an annoyed shrug. "That was all!" She was beginning to realize why her mother had been so tense and irritable lately. Mrs. Wolsky wasn't much fun to talk to.

"Hello, girls! We're home!"

"About time!" Jessica called from the patio, where she was sweeping up stray pieces of bologna.

Mr. Wakefield stepped through the doorway. "I hear we're switching places. So who's taking over for me at the office tomorrow morning?"

Jessica's heart was beating strangely. She and Elizabeth exchanged panicked looks.

Mr. Wakefield laughed. "Just kidding." He smiled and stretched. "I have to say, this is one of the best evenings I've had in a long time. I could get into being a kid again."

Mrs. Wakefield appeared on the patio next to him. "Oh, hi, girls. I think we should make this switch permanent."

"You do?" Elizabeth looked up from the garbage bag she was filling with leftover tomato slices.

Mrs. Wakefield laughed. "Oh, yes. We had such a time. First we climbed the jungle gym. Then we did the swings for a while."

"You did?" Jessica tried to imagine her mother on the swings.

"We even tried the seesaw," Mrs. Wakefield continued.

Mr. Wakefield shook his head and laughed. "It's been, what, thirty years since I last rode one of those."

"None of my friends were around, were they?" Jessica asked, a hollow feeling inside her.

Mr. and Mrs. Wakefield gave each other amused smiles. "I don't think so, dear," Mrs. Wakefield said. "Then we stopped by Casey's for ice cream. Anyway, I think I'll turn in. Good night, one and all."

Elizabeth and Jessica looked at each other. "Hey, wait a minute!" Jesica called out. "What about helping us clean up this mess?"

Mrs. Wakefield looked over the patio. "Oh, I don't know," she said, shaking her head and pressing her hand to her forehead. "I'm just so tired, and I need my beauty sleep."

Jessica frowned. Once again, her mother's comment sounded annoyingly familiar, but she decided to ignore it. "Mom!" she demanded. "You *have* to help."

"I guess there is a little bit of garbage," Mrs. Wakefield agreed with a sigh. "Oh, all right. Tell me what to do and I'll do it."

"A little bit of garbage? *That's* the understatement of the century," Jessica grumbled. She went into the kitchen and found a damp cloth for her mother. "Here."

Mrs. Wakefield took the cloth and frowned at it. "What am I supposed to do with this?"

"Oh, for goodness sakes, Mom," Elizabeth said impatiently, "just wash the picnic table." She turned back to the tomatoes.

Mrs. Wakefield sat on the bench. Dropping one corner of the rag onto the table, she brushed a few crumbs onto the deck. "You know, Ned," she said brightly to her husband, "I was thinking we should have an evening down at the beach tomorrow."

"That's a great idea!" Jessica commented. She loved the beach. She filled the dustpan with crumbs and dumped them into Elizabeth's garbage bag. "Maybe we should bring the volleyball."

"I beg your pardon?" Mrs. Wakefield said. She set the rag down and put on a huffy voice. "I was having a private conversation with Ned. You're not invited. Some of my friends might be there, and what would *they* think?"

Jessica bristled. Her mother's comments were starting to get to her.

Elizabeth threw away the pickle slices. "Mom,

please keep working. There's lots to do."

"Oh, is there?" Mrs. Wakefield's hand flew up to her forehead. "Oh, you're right! I just keep forgetting. You know how that goes, don't you, Jessica? You get to talking, and then you forget to do the job you're supposed to be doing." She twirled her hair with her fingers as she spoke. The rag lay bunched up on the table. "I'm sorry. I guess it just goes along with being a kid."

"Uh, yeah, right," Jessica said, sweeping up a few more crumbs. But crumbs kept falling around Mrs. Wakefield's feet. Jessica glanced at her mother, who was sitting on the bench, a dreamy expression on her face. "Mom, please don't dump the crumbs on the floor. I just swept there, and now I have to sweep it all over again— Mom!"

Mrs. Wakefield leaped up and looked embarrassed. "Excuse me, girls. I was thinking about something else, so I just couldn't concentrate on cleaning up," she said spacily brushing some more crumbs onto the floor.

"Oh, good grief, Mom!" Jessica exclaimed. "You're just making a mess! Why don't you just go to bed and let us take care of the cleanup!"

Mrs. Wakefield stood up and stretched. "Great idea, Jessica. I'm *beat*. Let's go, Ned."

Jessica looked at her mother in shock. "Aren't you even going to say thank you?"

"Thank you," Mrs. Wakefield said. "But what are moms for?"

*   *   *

Elizabeth looked at her bedside clock in the darkened room. Ten forty-five, and the music was still pounding through the house.

If you could call it music.

She got out of bed for what seemed like the twelfth time and padded into the hall. "Jessica?" she called. There was no point in whispering—it wouldn't be heard. "Are you still awake?"

A hollow laugh came through the darkness. "What do you think?"

"Do you want to tell her this time, or should I?"

Jessica sighed. "Let's both do it." Wearing a purple nightgown, she came out into the hall. "'You can't hide your lyin' eyes,'" she mimicked, shaking her head. "What kind of music is that?"

"Old," Elizabeth said.

"From the Dark Ages," Jessica put in. She rapped on their parents' door.

"Come in!" their mother called.

When the girls pushed the door open, Elizabeth stepped back in alarm. Mr. and Mrs. Wakefield, in pajamas, were standing by the bed—dancing. An old tape player was blasting the song about "your lying eyes."

"Mom!" Jessica cried.

"Daddy!" Elizabeth called. "Please turn it down!"

"We don't want to listen to seventies music all night!" Jessica continued, yelling above the roar of the tape player.

"What's that?" Mrs. Wakefield cupped her hand over her ear. "I can't hear you!"

"Turn the music down!" Jessica bellowed.

"Oh, is that all?" Mrs. Wakefield asked. She reached over and turned the volume down a notch. A new song began: *"'I remember when rock was young . . .'"*

"Lower!" Elizabeth gestured. Her mother frowned and lowered the volume one more notch. "Please, Mom. We can't sleep!"

"Oh, come on, girls," their mother shouted back. "We listen to your music! Listen to ours! Come dance with us!"

"No, thanks!" Jessica yelled angrily. "Just turn it down!"

"But the next song is my favorite!" their father cried.

"TURN DOWN THAT TAPE PLAYER THIS INSTANT!" Jessica demanded. Her father turned the volume to a normal level.

"Sheesh, where's your sense of fun, girls?" Mrs. Wakefield asked.

"Don't you know it's almost eleven o'clock at night?" Elizabeth demanded.

Mrs. Wakefield folded her arms. "I know that if I were a mother, I'd let my daughters play their music just as loud as they wanted."

"Well—well—you're not a mother," Jessica stammered, stalking out of the room.

Five

"So what do we do now?" Jessica asked on Friday morning.

The twins were standing on Mrs. Wolsky's sun-porch—which was completely bare. It looked as though no one had ever set foot there before, only there wasn't any dust, either.

"I don't know," Elizabeth said, sinking down onto the floor. "I don't know what we *can* do."

Jessica placed her hands on her hips. "What's with you, Lizzie?" she said. "*I'm* supposed to be the one who's always trying to get out of working, not you."

Elizabeth sighed. "Well, yeah, but this is—"

"This is just a tiny little setback," Jessica finished, pulling her sister up from the floor. "Don't worry, it'll all work out. Promise. Piece of cake."

"Every time you say 'piece of cake,' I feel like I'm getting a heart attack," Elizabeth said gloomily.

"Elizabeth!" Jessica scolded her. "Let's check out the rest of the house. That should give us some ideas, anyway. She said she'd be 'leaving for the weekend,'" she quoted with a sniff. "We've got plenty of time."

"All right," Elizabeth said at last. "It's better than doing nothing."

Mmm, seven o'clock, Mrs. Wakefield thought sleepily when she opened her eyes that morning. *I think I'll go back to sleep.* She could hear Jessica downstairs, arguing with Steven about emptying the garbage. *Better you than me*, Mrs. Wakefield thought with satisfaction as she drifted back to sleep. When she woke again, the clock read 10:15 and the house was quiet.

Mrs. Wakefield got up, leaving her bed unmade. Once down in the kitchen, she rummaged through the pantry and found a package of sugar doughnuts. Perfect! Mrs. Wakefield tore open the box and pulled one out.

Mmmmm, she thought, biting into the doughnut and sitting down at the table. *Much better than cereal. I should do this every day.* The best part about sugar doughnuts, she realized, was all the crumbs. When you were a kid you didn't have to worry about things like crumbs.

Mrs. Wakefield finished her doughnut and

helped herself to another, leaving the box open for the twins to put away. She stretched and smiled to herself. This was the life!

Now to plan out the day. Mrs. Wakefield reached for a pad and pencil. For fun, she wrote down "Groceries," "Paying Bills," and "Laundry" and crossed all three out with bold strokes. Elizabeth and Jessica didn't have to take on those responsibilities, so why should she?

Then she wrote "Mrs. Wolsky." This time, Mrs. Wakefield hesitated. She put her pencil down and chewed thoughtfully on her doughnut. Elizabeth and Jessica were hardly professional decorators. And what would happen to her business if the girls couldn't come through? *Is it fair to anybody to give the twins this responsibility?*

Mrs. Wakefield picked up the pencil and sketched a big question mark next to Mrs. Wolsky's name. Suddenly she had the glimmer of an idea. "Yes," she murmured out loud. "That might just do the trick." Smiling to herself, Mrs. Wakefield crossed out the question mark and replaced it with an exclamation point.

The rest of the list was easy. She'd start with Elizabeth's media-class project. Padding into the living room, Mrs. Wakefield settled down with the remote control. *Click.*

"Up and down and stretch those legs!" Aerobics! Mrs. Wakefield pressed the remote again. *Click.* "I couldn't believe how clean my dishes got when I tried—" *Click. Click. Click.* Mrs. Wakefield smiled to herself again. Channel surfing was quite an invention. *Click.* No wonder Jessica enjoyed it so much. She clicked past several game shows, commercials, and weather reports and a black-and-white movie before settling on the Phyllis Hartley Show. The famous talk show host was doing an hour-long program on "People Who Love Their Pets More Than Their Kids." She put a blank tape in the VCR and used the remote to activate it. Then she clicked to the proper channel. This was a cinch. She'd let the VCR record the program now and watch it later. After all, she had other things to do.

First, Jessica's pledge form for the Rollerblade-a-Thon. Where would it be? Mrs. Wakefield walked into Jessica's extremely untidy room. Shuddering at the mess, she forced herself to think about the pledge form. *If I were Jessica, where would I put it? I know—I bet it's under the bed.*

Mrs. Wakefield dropped to her knees and gingerly lifted the edge of Jessica's comforter. Reaching down, she saw an old shirt, a videotape marked *Days of Turmoil* in Jessica's handwriting, a lot of dust, and a piece of paper. *That's it!* Mrs. Wakefield thought triumphantly. She was even beginning to think like a kid.

On the way out the door, Mrs. Wakefield checked to make sure the VCR was still taping. Sure enough, the display was glowing. "And the next day," one of the guests on the program was saying, "I told my children to follow the German shepherd's example. If they didn't, I said, the dog would just get a bigger allowance."

Satisfied, Mrs. Wakefield walked next door, Jessica's pledge form in hand. No one was home. Two doors down, the house was empty, too. Finally, the third neighbor answered the door.

"Good morning," she said brightly. "I'm Alice Wakefield from a few houses down. I'm Rollerblading on Sunday to raise money for children's charities, and—"

"Rollerblading?" The woman who answered the door stared at Mrs. Wakefield. "You're kidding me, right?"

"Oh, no, not at all," Mrs. Wakefield assured her. "It's for a good cause. It's a three-mile course, and you sign up to sponsor me for a certain amount for every mile. Let me show you." She held out Jessica's sponsor list.

"'Jessica Wakefield,'" the woman read. "Thought you said your name was Alice." She laughed and kept on reading. "'Age: twelve.' Twelve years old, hey? You don't look a day over eleven." Laughing uproariously, the woman shut the door before Mrs. Wakefield could begin to explain.

"Well, thanks for your support," Mrs. Wakefield said, glaring at the door.

Things didn't get much better farther down the block. Either no one was home, or the person who answered the door refused to take Mrs. Wakefield seriously.

Mrs. Wakefield sighed wearily. She was beginning to feel embarrassed about asking for pledges. She was also beginning to realize that Jessica was a lot better at it than she was.

A minute or so after Mrs. Wakefield rounded the corner, another figure followed: a tall, brown-haired boy with a video camera pressed to his eye. As Mrs. Wakefield rang the first doorbell on the block, Steven crept as close as he dared and aimed the camera right at his mother.

"Good morning," Mrs. Wakefield said, smiling as broadly as she could when the door opened. "I'm doing some charity work and I wondered if you'd like to make a donation."

Steven couldn't quite hear the response, but he kept filming.

"No, charity work," he could hear his mother explain. "It's for the cancer ward of the children's hospital." She thrust out the pledge sheet. Steven noticed that she had folded down the top, so Jessica's name was hidden. "As you see, most people are pledging cnly two or three dollars per mile, and I'm hoping that you— Beg your pardon?"

Steven shifted position to try to get more of his mother's face. He wished the person she was talking to would come out onto the steps and speak more clearly.

"Well, the handwriting looks childish because it is. I've mostly been asking my daughters and their friends so far," Mrs. Wakefield explained. The person at the door said something. "Yes— Well . . ." Mrs. Wakefield tossed her hands into the air and pasted a grin on her face. "It's just that children are so busy these days, I thought I'd handle it myself instead of asking them to do the work— Yes, yes— Oh. I see." The door closed.

Mrs. Wakefield slowly walked toward the sidewalk. Then, as Steven filmed away, an idea seemed to come to her. She stopped at the mailbox, leaned the pledge sheet against it, and copied something down. With a grin, she went on to the next house. This time she didn't even bother to ring the doorbell. She just checked the mailbox and wrote on the pledge form. Around the block she went, stopping at every few houses.

And Steven kept right on taping.

"This place is really neat," Jessica said with excitement.

She and Elizabeth were exploring Mrs. Wolsky's house, which was fancy and elegant. It was also extremely tidy. Everything was polished, smooth, gleaming. "I could live here."

Elizabeth looked at her sister skeptically. "Are you kidding? I somehow can't picture you in a place this spotless. You'd mess it up in a flash."

Jessica breezed farther into the house, ignoring Elizabeth's comment. "See, isn't this great?" she said, pointing to an old-fashioned wardrobe.

"Look at the way that wood is carved."

"It *is* pretty," Elizabeth admitted. "But it looks *too* clean—like a museum or something. It gives me the creeps."

"Well, it gives me some ideas about decorating the sunporch," Jessica said. "Let's go back home and talk them over."

"Ugh," Elizabeth said as she and Jessica entered their kitchen through the glass doors. "Someone forgot to clean up after herself." She looked meaningfully at her twin.

"Not me," Jessica said, glancing at the remains of the sugar doughnuts.

"We're going to have to sit down with Mom and have a talk," Elizabeth said with a sigh. "Hey, what's that noise?"

Together they walked into the living room. On the television, Phyllis Hartley was talking to her guest, an amazed expression on her face. "So, ma'am, you're telling me that if your cat and your son were drowning, you'd choose to save the cat?"

"If the son's anything like Steven, I don't blame her," Jessica murmured.

"Well, Miss Hartley," the guest replied, "that situation couldn't possibly come up. I'd never let my cat near the swimming pool."

"Mom must be taping this show," Elizabeth said, staring at the VCR.

"Not exactly." Jessica giggled and pointed to the

left-hand side of the VCR display. "See this?" she asked, indicating a few numbers in the corner. "Mom isn't recording this channel. She's recording channel 73 onto the tape in the VCR instead."

Elizabeth smiled. "What's on Channel Seventy-three?"

Jessica chuckled. "We don't get it on our cable system. The tape's going to wind up with nothing but static."

"Maybe we should tell her," Elizabeth said. "Or fix it for her."

Jessica smiled slyly. "Well, we *could*," she began, "but I've always heard you should let kids fix their own mistakes."

"You know," Elizabeth said just as slyly, "I've heard the very same thing."

Six

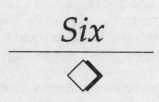

Mrs. Wakefield walked up to her house, humming happily to herself. It was only Saturday afternoon, and everything was settled.

As far as Mrs. Wolsky was concerned, Mrs. Wakefield just had a phone call to make. *Sometime before dinner would be fine*, she told herself.

And as for the Rollerblade-a-thon, Mrs. Wakefield had collected another $75 for the children's hospital without breaking a sweat. With a slight twinge of guilt, she looked at the pledge sheet in her hand. The people whose names appeared on the paper would be very surprised to learn that they were sponsoring her. Especially since most of them had never even heard of Mrs. Wakefield.

"But they'll never find out!" Mrs. Wakefield said aloud as she bounded into the house. Her plan was perfect. Jessica would be amazed at how quickly she'd gotten all those pledges. And the children's hospital wouldn't suffer, because Mrs. Wakefield would donate the $75 herself. Yes, it was much easier than going door-to-door.

Jessica came to the top of the stairs, a smile on her face. "What won't who find out?"

"Oh—nothing." Mrs. Wakefield wasn't about to let Jessica in on her little secret. "I got you another seventy-five dollars in pledges, honey." Casually she held the form out to Jessica.

"That's nice." Jessica didn't seem to notice. "Were you watching TV in there, Mom?"

"Yes, I was," Mrs. Wakefield said. "Kids are allowed to watch on days when there's no school, aren't they?"

"Sure," Jessica said. "I was just checking. Say, Mom, next time you go out, leave us a note, OK? We like to know where you are at all times."

Mrs. Wakefield's face fell. "Oh. Sorry. I'll try to remember."

"Please," Jessica said, smiling again. "It isn't because we don't trust you—"

"It's because we love you!" Elizabeth's voice came from inside the bedroom. Laughing hysterically, Jessica darted inside the room and pulled the door shut.

I guess I've trained them well, Mrs. Wakefield thought as she went into the living room.

Phyllis Hartley was still on. *Good.* Mrs. Wakefield

plumped herself into the easy chair. Making sure no one was looking, she reached out her legs and rested her feet on the couch. This was the life, all right. Mrs. Wakefield considered going to the kitchen and getting a handful of chips, but she thought maybe she'd wait for the commercial.

Then she remembered there weren't any chips in the house, anyway.

"So tell us about the Jacuzzi you built for your dog," Phyllis Hartley was asking a very tall man, when suddenly the VCR clicked a couple of times. *Oops,* Mrs. Wakefield thought, *I forgot to check how much time was left on the tape before I put it in.* She looked at the clock. Three minutes remaining on the show. *It won't matter if I miss three minutes,* she thought. Finding the remote control, she clicked the rewind button.

Nothing happened.

Mrs. Wakefield aimed the remote again and pushed the button once more. Still nothing.

"Well, my children aren't nearly as well behaved as the dog," the very tall man was saying. Frowning, Mrs. Wakefield aimed the remote directly at the man and clicked the rewind button five times. *That should do the trick,* she said to herself.

Only it didn't. Mrs. Wakefield sat forward and clicked the rewind button once more. Then she tried the play button, the fast-forward button, and the volume buttons, just to be on the safe side. "THE DOG DESERVES ONE, AND THE CHILDREN

DON'T," the very tall man was yelling.

"Mom!" Elizabeth's voice came over the blaring TV set.

Mrs. Wakefield got up and went over to the VCR. *How does this thing work, anyway?* she asked herself. Dropping to the floor, she reached for a knob on the TV set and turned it sharply to the left. Phyllis Hartley's face turned bright blue. Wrong knob. She tried another one. The very tall man suddenly became three very tall men, each one bouncing up and down on his chair. Wrong knob again. Now three Phyllis Hartleys faced the camera. Bouncing up and down, they all screamed, "THIS HAS BEEN THE PHYLLIS HARTLEY SHOW."

"Mo-om!"

Mrs. Wakefield found another knob and twisted it. Good. The three Phyllis Hartley voices dropped to a whisper. "Monday morning," they said, looking meaningfully out at their audience, "we'll feature 'People over Thirty Who Have Learned to Program Their VCRs.' See you then!" The three studio audiences in the background bounced up and down, clapping enthusiastically. The orchestra began the theme music for *The Phyllis Hartley Show.*

Feeling a little desperate, Mrs. Wakefield turned her attention to the VCR. She pushed a button and flipped a switch. The TV picture spun out of control. Still, the tape in the VCR refused to rewind. She ejected it and examined the cassette. It looked fine to her. Feeding it back in, she pressed every button she could think of. Nothing happened.

Mrs. Wakefield stood up and clenched her fists, getting ready to kick the television set.

"Hey, cool it, Mom," Steven said, suddenly appearing in the room. "What's going on?"

"Steven!" Mrs. Wakefield said, delighted. "Just the person I wanted to see."

"Hey, don't kick the TV, Mom, OK?" Steven was worried. "There are still some basketball playoff games coming up." Besides eating, Steven loved nothing more than basketball.

Mrs. Wakefield forced a laugh. "I wasn't going to break the TV, honey." *At least I don't think so*, she added to herself. "But you can help me. You're really good with VCRs." She motioned for Steven to sit down.

"Is that Steven?" Jessica's voice floated down from the top of the stairs. "Send him on up! We have plenty of stuff for him to do!"

Steven's lip curled in disgust.

"Just a minute, girls," Mrs. Wakefield called. "He needs to help me with one thing. Then he'll be right up."

"Well, you better send him *right* up!" Jessica insisted.

Steven shot her a look of alarm. "But I have this volleyball game at the beach—"

Mrs. Wakefield clutched Steven's arm. "Listen," she said in a low voice so the girls couldn't hear, "this is serious. Help me out and I'll cover for you.

I'll say I misunderstood them or something."

Steven shrugged. "Why not? They do it all the time, anyway." He knelt down and ejected the tape. Shaking his head, he gave a low whistle. "Boy, you really messed this up."

"Can you get it to work?" Mrs. Wakefield asked hopefully.

Steven just stared at her.

"Sorry," Mrs. Wakefield said. "I guess that was a stupid question."

Steven began turning knobs and pushing buttons. After a moment, Mrs. Wakefield heard the humming sound made by a rewinding tape. "Oh, great," she said with relief. "Thank you so much, Steven."

"Don't you want to check and make sure that the tape recorded what you wanted it to?" Steven asked.

Mrs. Wakefield frowned. "Doesn't it automatically record what's on the TV?"

Steven rolled his eyes. "No way. If you leave the TV/VCR button tuned to UHF, and you don't remember to change DISPLAY so it matches the number of the channel you're watching, then you get a different channel. Unless you also forgot to put the channel selector on three," he added.

"Oh," Mrs. Wakefield said, nodding as if she understood. "It seems a little complicated."

"Complicated?" Steven repeated, narrowing his eyes. "This is one of the simplest models on the market." Stopping the tape, Steven grabbed the remote and pushed a sequence of buttons. "Let's see how you did," he said. The TV screen went blank. Then static took its place.

"Oh, dear," Mrs. Wakefield said.

Steven sighed loudly. "You didn't do it right, Mom," he informed her. "Look. The display has to match the channel you're watching." He clicked another button on the remote. The number "73" leaped into view above the static. "See?"

"So I recorded Channel Seventy-three by accident?" Mrs. Wakefield said.

"No, you recorded Channel Seventy-three and looked at it in a mirror," Steven said sarcastically. He ran his fingers through his hair irritably. "I bet Steven Starholtz never had to put up with this. I bet Steven Starholtz's parents could operate a VCR."

"Well, could you help me record another show?" Mrs. Wakefield asked timidly.

"Steven!" Jessica shouted from upstairs. "This instant!"

"Tell me what to do, and I'll follow the directions." Mrs. Wakefield lowered her voice as she saw Steven look around frantically.

Steven quickly listed the steps in order, then looked at her skeptically. "Maybe you should write all that down or something?"

"I don't need to," Mrs. Wakefield assured him. It had sounded pretty simple, at that. "Now, go!"

Two doors banged at once: Elizabeth's upstairs

and the screen door leading outside. Elizabeth came down into the living room, a worried look on her face. "Where's Steven, Mom?" she asked.

Mrs. Wakefield pretended to be shocked. "Steven? He left—for the beach, I think. Something about a volleyball game." She tapped her cheek with her forefinger. "Why? Is something the matter?"

"Mom!" Elizabeth put her hands on her hips. "We asked you to send him right upstairs."

"You did?" Mrs. Wakefield got up from the floor. "I thought you said you needed to see him— later on today."

Elizabeth rolled her eyes. "Mom, you're not a very good liar."

"No?" Mrs. Wakefield sat down again, embarrassed. "Sorry if I messed things up for you. But if you'll excuse me, I really have to get to work on my school project."

Elizabeth glared at her mother for a moment while Mrs. Wakefield tried to look innocent. At last Elizabeth dropped her gaze and started on upstairs. "Please clean up the mess on the table before you do anything else," she said, closing the door to her room.

"Well, it wasn't mine!" Mrs. Wakefield snapped back. No doubt about it, she was enjoying being a kid again.

Now what did Steven say to do? Mrs. Wakefield wondered when she was alone with the VCR. *Let's see.* Carefully she rewound the tape all the way to the beginning. So far, so good. She flipped channels till she found another talk show. The topic was "Parents Who Do Their Children's Homework Assignments for Them." Channel 18. Check.

Now came the hard part. Mrs. Wakefield remembered that the first step was "Have the display match the channel." Or was it "Make sure the channel selector is tuned to 3?" Come to think of it, was the channel selector supposed to be tuned to 3 or 4? She couldn't quite recall Steven's instructions.

Maybe she should have taken notes.

Mrs. Wakefield racked her brain. There was something about the TV/VCR button, wasn't there? She looked at it. It was set at "UHF." That couldn't be right, could it? She flipped the switch to "CABLE." That sounded better. After all, they had a cable system. Cheering up, Mrs. Wakefield found the "Display" key on the remote. A green "12" lit up the corner of the screen.

Wait. That didn't make sense. Steven had said to get the channel selector to match the display, and the channel selector was set at 18. Wasn't it? Or was it supposed to be on 3?

Uh-oh.

Frantically, Mrs. Wakefield began clicking buttons.

"I think it's going to be all right. For now," Jessica told Elizabeth, her ear pressed to the bedroom door.

"We could ground her for using bad language," Elizabeth suggested, also listening as her mother called the VCR various names.

Jessica giggled. "This is great. It's obvious that she can't get the VCR to work. And it's driving her crazy."

"Do you think Steven gave her bad directions?" Elizabeth asked.

"I wish!" Jessica replied. "But I doubt it. I bet she just figured she could learn it like that." She snapped her fingers to demonstrate. "And she can't."

Elizabeth nodded. "But what if she asks him again? I mean, I don't want her to have too easy a time with this. Especially since she already got the pledges for the Rollerblade-a-thon."

"No problem," Jessica said breezily. "We'll think of something."

Elizabeth sighed. "The sunporch is where we really need to think of something." She picked up a decorating magazine from the pile on her bed. "Do you like this design?"

"No," Jessica said immediately.

Elizabeth shook her head. "Good. Neither do I."

Jessica picked up another magazine and began leafing through it. For a few minutes the girls sat flipping pages, absorbed in the designs they saw.

"Nothing in there," Elizabeth said, laying down a magazine on her bed.

"Here, look at this!" Jessica said excitedly,

thrusting her magazine at Elizabeth. "This one's pretty neat. It might work."

Elizabeth looked down at the page. The furniture was fancy and glittery. "I don't know, Jess," she began.

"I knew you wouldn't like it," Jessica said, grabbing the magazine back. "But I do. And so would Mrs. Wolsky."

Elizabeth nodded. The furniture in the picture did remind her a lot of Mrs. Wolsky's house. "All right," she said, swallowing hard. "I guess we should find out some things about the designs. Like how much it costs."

"That's just a minor detail," Jessica assured her sister. "Let's see. 'Prices appear on page seventy-nine,'" she read. "How much does furniture cost, anyway?" she asked, as she flipped to the proper page.

"I think it's a lot," Elizabeth said anxiously.

"Well, if I can get seventy-five dollars in pledges for the Rollerblade-a-thon in less than a week, how long can it take to get a couple hundred bucks for furniture?" Jessica asked. She ran her finger down the price list. "Let's see, page forty-four. 'Total cost of entire sunporch set—ten thousand dollars . . .'" she read, her voice trailing off.

The girls looked at each other in dismay.

"Ten thousand dollars?" Elizabeth gasped.

"How can Mom afford it?" Jessica scowled. "I sure hope she doesn't have to pay it out of her own pocket!"

"Well, we certainly can't," Elizabeth said decisively. "Anyway, I told you that it wasn't a good design. Let's keep looking."

Jessica gave in. "All right." She marked the place in the magazine, just in case.

For a few more minutes, the girls thumbed through the magazines.

"Here's something, Jess," Elizabeth said at last, holding out a picture to her sister.

Jessica looked at it critically. "That isn't much. It's just a couple of chairs, a tiny table, and a lamp. There isn't even an area rug."

"I know," Elizabeth said, "but—"

"The chairs don't even look comfortable," Jessica went on, "and it doesn't match Mrs. Wolsky's style at all."

"True," Elizabeth admitted. "But the design's probably cheap—there isn't much furniture."

"Hmm, good point," Jessica said. "Look up the price."

"Let's see," Elizabeth murmured as she flipped to the right page. When she found the price, she slammed the magazine shut. She looked at her sister gravely. "Would you believe eight thousand dollars?" she asked Jessica weakly.

"For two uncomfortable chairs, a table, and a lamp?" Jessica cried. "That's ridiculous!"

Elizabeth faced her twin and drummed her fingers on her comforter. "This isn't going to work," she said. "We should give up right now."

"No way!" Jessica told her. She looked at her watch. "I think we should go down to the beach and talk to Steven about not helping Mom with the VCR. The least we can do is make sure that Mom has as hard a time as we're having."

Seven

"Which way do you think Steven went?" Jessica asked Elizabeth once the twins had arrived at the beach and locked their bikes together.

"Let's try to the left," Elizabeth suggested, sighting down the beach. "I think I see some volleyball players over there."

"OK," Jessica agreed.

The twins found Steven just as he had served the last point of the match. *Good*, Jessica thought. *He'll be in a decent mood.*

"Well, if it isn't Mom and Other-Mom!" he said, raising his eyebrows at Jessica and Elizabeth.

"Steven," Jessica said, trying to imitate the tone her mother usually took with him, "we have to have a little talk."

"We need your help," Elizabeth put in.

Steven laughed. "With that list of jobs you put together for me? Not a chance. Abraham Lincoln freed the slaves. Or hadn't you heard?"

"Sheesh, it's not like you've done that many of those chores," Jessica said, exasperated.

"Steven, we don't want you to help Mom with the VCR, OK?" Elizabeth cut in.

"Too late. I already did," Steven pointed out. "The only man alive who can teach his mother how to program the VCR! Huzzah, huzzah, huzzah."

"Dream on," Jessica said sarcastically.

"She didn't understand your directions," Elizabeth explained.

"She's hopeless," Jessica added. "And we want to keep her that way."

Steven lowered his hands and looked from one twin to the other. "Even by your standards, that sounds kind of mean."

Jessica caught her sister's embarrassed look. "Oh, come on, Lizzie, don't let him make you feel guilty." She turned to Steven. "It's for a good cause, believe me."

Steven frowned. "What will you give me if I do it?"

Jessica drew the list of chores out of her pocket. "This is yours if you promise not to show Mom how to use the VCR again." She waved the list in front of his face, the way she'd once seen a magician hypnotize someone on TV. *Who knows,* she told herself, *maybe he'll fall under my spell.*

"You can't program the VCR for her, either,"

Elizabeth hastened to add, getting back into the swing of things.

Steven snatched the list from Jessica's hand and studied it. Then he stuffed it into his pocket. "All right—that's a start. What else do I get?"

"You want *more*?" Jessica asked indignantly. "You have some—"

Elizabeth put her hand on Jessica's arm. "Actually, Steven, I was thinking—have you ever done anything for us before? For free, that is?"

"Not on your life," Steven said proudly, kicking a little sand on the twins.

"And have you ever done anything nice for Mom? Just because, I mean?" Elizabeth went on.

Steven shrugged. "Yeah. I guess so."

"So with us and Mom switching places," Elizabeth explained, "it's like Mom's now your sister and we're your mother. So we're the ones you should be helping." She grinned at Steven hopefully.

Steven smiled. "Cute, kid. Definitely cute. But I have a better idea."

"What is it?" Jessica asked suspiciously.

"Nothing much," Steven said. "I just want your help with a movie project."

"And if we help you, you'll promise not to help Mom?" Jessica wanted to know.

"That's the deal," Steven assured them.

"I don't know," Elizabeth said with a frown. "What do we have to do?"

"I'll let you know at home," Steven said. "You don't have to act or anything. Do we have a deal? Take it or leave it."

The twins looked at each other. "All right," Jessica said at last. But just in case, she crossed her fingers behind her back.

"Anyone home?" Steven shouted, swinging open the door. He marched into the living room, the twins behind him.

The only sound was static coming from the TV.

"Mom's gone, and she didn't leave a note," Elizabeth complained.

"She's got the TV tuned to channel 73 again," Jessica said with satisfaction. "But what's going on with the VCR?" She crossed the room for a closer look. "Steven, come take a look. This is bizarre."

Steven joined his sister. He rubbed his eyes and stared.

The VCR was glowing. It seemed to be set on both rewind and record. The time display, blinking furiously, said it was exactly 15:72 P.M. "Boy, did she mess this up," Jessica said.

"Look at this tape!" Steven said. He picked up a rental video and stared at it. The tape looped out from the cassette and halfway around the room. As Steven began to wind up the ends, he realized the tape had been broken in three places. "It looks like the VCR's eaten it," he said slowly.

"She's going to have one huge fine," Jessica said.

Steven picked a few more tapes up off the floor. "This one's Dad's," he said with a frown. "Remember, the tape of all those PBS documentaries that no one else ever watches? 'The Private Life of the Rabbit,' that kind of thing?" He shook his head. "I sure hope she hasn't damaged this one. Dad'll hit the roof." He punched a few buttons on the VCR and inserted Mr. Wakefield's tape.

Static.

Steven groaned and put in the next tape from the pile. "This one was that volleyball game I taped when I was just starting out as a moviemaker," he told the girls as he waited for the tape to rewind. "If she's messed this one up, I'll—" Pressing the play button, Steven held his breath.

Static again.

"She's taped over everything," Elizabeth said in amazement, looking through the six or seven videos in the stack.

"No wonder she left the house," Jessica remarked. "Good thing I left my *Days of Turmoil* tape under my bed."

Angrily, Steven shut down the VCR. "How can I be a famous filmmaker if my work gets destroyed?" he said, throwing his hands in the air.

"Suffering builds character," Jessica said slyly.

Steven switched the TV off, groaning again. If he were president, he'd introduce a law that banned parents from touching electronic equipment.

*   *   *

Where did I put those tomatoes? Steven wondered. *Oh, yeah—bottom drawer.* He had led Jessica and Elizabeth into the kitchen in order to show them how they could fill their part of the bargain. Yanking the refrigerator drawer open, he began pulling the tomatoes out. "When Steven Starholtz was a boy," he said, "he got his mother to cook a cherry pie in a pressure cooker till it exploded."

"Yuck," Elizabeth said. "Why would he do that?"

"What's a pressure cooker?" Jessica wanted to know.

Steven rolled his eyes. His sisters could be so dense. "It's like a little oven that cooks food by putting pressure on it," Steven explained. "And he did it so he could film the red stuff oozing down all over the walls of the kitchen, just like blood. Why else?"

"Double yuck," Elizabeth said, making a face.

"So where do we come in?" Jessica asked.

"Well, since we don't have a pressure cooker," Steven began, "I've been thinking I can get the same effect with tomatoes in the microwave. That's why I went out and bought all these tomatoes." He shut the refrigerator and indicated the pile on the kitchen counter.

"So that's where they all came from," Elizabeth said.

"See, a tomato has a skin, so the heat that builds

up inside can't get out," Steven went on. "I figure the microwaves will build up till they pop the whole tomato. Then I stick my camera in, and the rest is history. Instant blood!"

Elizabeth looked worried. "What if the microwave explodes?"

"It won't," Steven assured her, hoping he was right. "But see, this is the problem. Mom would never let me do it." Jessica nodded in agreement. "But now that you're my moms, you will! Right?" Steven flashed them a toothy grin.

"You bet!" Jessica said, quickly clamping a hand over Elizabeth's mouth. "Let's do it."

"Don't blame me if anything blows up," Elizabeth muttered when Jessica released her.

Steven got the camera ready as Jessica started loading tomatoes into the microwave. "Should I just make rows to put them in, or should I stack them?" she asked.

"Try making a pyramid," Steven said.

Elizabeth moved closer. "Just don't set the timer for more than about five minutes, OK?"

"All right, Mom," Steven said cheerfully, checking to make sure the lighting was right. He found the best angle and stood back while Jessica loaded the microwave. *This is going to be so great*, he thought.

Jessica stacked up ten tomatoes, closed the door of the microwave, and set the timer. "All clear!" she said, pressing the start button.

"Better stand back," Elizabeth warned her.

Through the glass door they could see the tomatoes heating up. "Now, remember, Jessica," Steven said, focusing through the lens, "when they start popping, open the door so I can stick the camera inside, OK?"

"OK," Jessica promised.

They had been recording for less than a minute when Mrs. Wakefield walked in. "What on earth are you doing?" she asked in alarm.

At that moment one of the tomatoes gave a dull *oomph*. Red tomato insides spurted out and onto the wall of the microwave.

"All *right*!" Jessica said, pumping her fist up in the air.

"What are you children doing to the microwave?" Mrs. Wakefield repeated in amazement.

"A lot less than you did to my volleyball tape," Steven grunted as another tomato popped open, and then another. Red stains appeared on the inside of the microwave door. Jessica quickly yanked it open, and Steven moved in for a close-up. "This is *terrific*!" he exulted.

"This is—" Mrs. Wakefield began, then broke off. She left the room while Steven continued to tape.

"Excellent," he said at last, shutting the camera down. "Thanks, shrimps."

"No problem. Just remember to give us credit when you become rich and famous," Jessica told him.

"And Steven," Elizabeth added, putting on her sunniest smile, "don't forget the other part of our bargain."

Steven grinned. "Trust me, kid," he told her, giving her an exaggerated wink, as he'd seen a character do in Steven Starholtz's latest film. "Trust me."

"May I come in?" Mrs. Wakefield sang outside Jessica's door at five o'clock that afternoon.

"Uh-oh," Jessica said to Elizabeth. "This doesn't sound good."

Elizabeth dropped the magazine she was holding and opened the door. "Hi, Mom," she said.

"Hello, dear," Mrs. Wakefield said, smiling broadly. "I just wanted to know what's for dinner tonight. It's almost time, you know."

"It is?" Jessica said.

"And since you girls are responsible for making it, I thought maybe you'd like to get a head start," Mrs. Wakefield continued.

Elizabeth and Jessica looked at each other in consternation. They had forgotten all about dinner.

"Dad will be working late, so it'll just be the four of us," Mrs. Wakefield went on. "I'm sure we can expect something very tasty. Well, I won't keep you. Steven's promised to show me how to operate the VCR." She winked at Elizabeth, who stared at her with her mouth wide open. "Toodle-oo!" Whistling to herself, she headed back down the stairs.

"What a total traitor!" Jessica burst out. "After

all we did for him, too!" She stood up and tossed one of her pillows onto the bed.

"Wait," Elizabeth said quickly. "Let's not jump to conclusions. I mean, he did sound pretty grateful for our help with the exploding tomatoes. Maybe he's got something up his sleeve."

The twins tiptoed to the top of the stairs and listened.

"You see, Mom, it's really very simple," Steven was saying. "All you have to do is put your new tape in without changing any of the channels or altering the display—assuming that the channel tuner is tuned to any channel besides five, seven, or thirty-eight, that is, because if it's tuned to any of those channels you'll only get static as long as the TV/VCR button stays in the off position."

"Oh," their mother replied doubtfully. "I guess I understand."

"No, no, no, Mom," Steven continued. "If you put the tape in like that, you could destroy the coaxial cable, which erases all the magnetism on the recording heads. You need to flick your wrist, like so."

The twins looked at each other and started giggling softly. "Good," Jessica said. "I wouldn't want to think that all my hard work with the tomatoes was for nothing!"

"See, the display mode has to be an even number to record a comedy," Steven said to his mother.

Mrs. Wakefield bit her lip. It was six o'clock, and

she was growing desperate. Nothing Steven was saying made any sense at all. Since she was no closer to having a tape than she had been that morning, she decided to put Plan B into action.

"Steven, dear," she interrupted, putting on a sweet smile. "Let's not worry about this anymore. Aren't you going out tonight?"

"Yeah—I'm going down to the beach with Cathy." Cathy Connors was Steven's girlfriend. Like him, she was a freshman at Sweet Valley High School.

"Well, you're going to want to tape the basketball game then," Mrs. Wakefield explained, crossing her fingers behind her back. *Not that there is a basketball game*, she reminded herself. *But if I can't learn to program the VCR, I'm just going to have to fool you into taping something for me.*

"Basketball game?" Steven asked, puzzled. "What basketball game?"

"You mean you don't know about tonight's game?" Mrs. Wakefield tried to sound amazed. "You didn't hear about it?"

"Who's playing?" Steven frowned at her.

Mrs. Wakefield thought hard. The Saints? No, that was a football team. "Um—the Lakers," she said. The L.A. Lakers. Of course!

"The Lakers," Steven repeated. "Mom, the Lakers didn't even make the playoffs this season."

Mrs. Wakefield laughed nervously. "Oh, did I say the Lakers? I meant the Bulls. That's right, the

Bulls. They're playing Houston." Cities were safer than team nicknames, she decided.

Steven just stared at her. "The Bulls were knocked out in the first round by the Hornets. And they wouldn't play Houston till the final, anyway. They're in different conferences. Where's the *TV Guide*?"

"I can't imagine," Mrs. Wakefield lied. *Honestly, how did kids get to be so smart?*

Just at that moment, Elizabeth came out of the kitchen, covered with dough and holding out the missing magazine. "I found this in the garbage can," she said sternly, "and the week isn't over yet! Who's responsible?"

"You sound just like Mom," Steven remarked, tearing the *TV Guide* out of her hands and flipping through to Friday's listings. "Just as I thought," he said. "No games tonight!" He stared at his mother. With horror, she watched the light beginning to dawn in his eyes. "I get it," he said slowly. "This was all a trick, wasn't it!"

"I'm sorry," Mrs. Wakefield began, turning bright red. "Please, Steven, I really—"

Steven rubbed his forehead and began to laugh. "Never mind, Mom. But I'll tell you something, that was a pretty good try." He got up off the floor. "It's exactly the kind of stunt the twins would pull, know what I mean?"

"Is that supposed to be an insult?" Elizabeth and Mrs. Wakefield asked him at the same time.

*　　　*　　　*

"Ta-da!" Elizabeth announced at seven thirty as she placed the pizza she and Jessica had made for dinner on the table.

Steven was already reaching for the pizza cutter. "Finally! I'm about to starve— Yuck!" He dropped the pizza cutter. "That looks completely disgusting. What'd you use to make it—chopped-up rubber tires?"

"Steven Wakefield!" Jessica protested. "We did the best we could."

"If that's the best, I'd sure hate to see the worst," Steven muttered. He helped himself to a slice and set it on his plate, frowning. "It's burned to a crisp."

"I guess it *is* a little overdone," Elizabeth admitted, blushing.

"And where's the cheese?" Steven demanded, pulling a chunk off his slice and waving it as he held it between his thumb and forefinger. "This looks like crust with a little bit of tomato sauce— period!"

"Oh, please, you're just being a baby. Anyone can see there's plenty of cheese on this pizza!" Jessica snapped back.

Elizabeth decided it wasn't a good time to explain that she had accidentally put all the cheese on one side of the pizza.

Their mother sighed. Helping herself to a slice, she looked at it carefully. "What kind of topping is this, anyway?"

"We had a little trouble with the toppings," Elizabeth confessed.

"Trouble?" Mrs. Wakefield asked, taking a small bite.

"Well, first we couldn't agree on anything," Elizabeth went on. "Then we decided on pepperoni, but we didn't have any pepperoni in the house, so I had to get on my bike and ride all the way down to the supermarket to buy some. It was a real zoo down there. Tons of people. I had to wait in line for a long time."

"But this doesn't look like pepperoni to me," Mrs. Wakefield said.

"That's because it isn't," Jessica jumped in. "She bought a really small package. Not enough to go around."

"Well, I tried!" Elizabeth said, glaring at her sister. "But pepperoni costs more than I thought it did, and I only had a couple of dollars."

"That's the kind of thing grown-ups go through every single day," Mrs. Wakefield reminded her, with a gentle smile.

"Not really," Jessica pointed out. "You have a checking account. We don't. You can also drive a car, Mom. We can't. I had to make two more trips to the store. On my bicycle! And you wonder why dinner was a little late?"

"Sorry, girls," Mrs. Wakefield said mischievously. "I guess in the future you'll just have to be more organized."

"Not only that—" Elizabeth began, but she bit her lip. She decided not to mention that the dishwasher hadn't been run, the microwave was full of tomatoes, and some idiot had left a sugar doughnut on the table. She cleared her throat. "Well, eat up, everybody," she said bleakly, looking from her mother to her brother.

"That's a laugh," Steven said, chewing a mouthful. "This stuff is completely inedible. Tastes just like cardboard."

Mrs. Wakefield was still studying her slice. "You never told me what kind of topping this is," she reminded the girls.

Elizabeth looked pleadingly at Jessica, who was concentrating on her food.

Elizabeth looked back at her mother and smiled brightly. "Tomatoes," she said cheerfully. "Yum! I just love tomatoes!"

Eight

◇

"Why is the sink plugged up?" Jessica demanded on Saturday morning.

"Beats me," Steven said, shrugging and wolfing down his fourth slice of toast.

Elizabeth looked up from her bowl of cereal, a concerned look on her face. "Who's used it so far this morning?"

"I was going to just now," Jessica said, scowling. "The water won't go down." She glanced sideways at her father.

Mr. Wakefield turned a page in his newspaper. "I haven't used the sink at all today."

"Steven?" Jessica said accusingly.

Steven shook his head. "Negative."

"And it can't be Mom," Elizabeth said, thoughtfully. "She isn't up yet. So it must be left over from yesterday." She tapped her finger against her chin. "Oops."

"What is it?" Jessica asked her.

"Did we run the disposal last night?" Elizabeth said.

Jessica shook her head and peered down the drain. "Four slices of pizza," she said bitterly. "No wonder nothing will go down."

"You threw out pizza?" Mr. Wakefield said, putting down the paper and looking curiously at the girls.

"This wasn't just any old pizza, Dad," Steven told him, smiling broadly. "This was genuine Jessica-and-Elizabeth Wakefield Brand Killer Pizza! They made it themselves, you know."

"Steven, the next time you play volleyball, why don't you use your head for the ball?" Jessica suggested.

"The advertising slogan should be 'If you want to know the truth: try to eat it, lose a tooth,'" Steven went on, paying no attention to his sister. "It supplies a hundred percent of your minimum daily requirement for rubber and charcoal. No—better make that two hundred percent. Which reminds me, what's for dinner tonight? Eggs à la Metal? Chicken Noodle Soap? Dad, you want to take me out to dinner?"

"Ste-ven!" Jessica said, picking up the bowl of cereal and aiming it at him threateningly.

Mr. Wakefield chuckled. "Come on, Steven. I'm

sure your sisters' cooking can't be as bad as all that."

"No?" Steven smirked. He swallowed the last bite of toast. "I'm out to make some movies. Anybody want to be the next Hollywood star?"

Jessica snorted. "Why don't you go film some ant colonies or something?"

"Don't call us, we'll call you," Steven said. He grabbed his movie camera and was out the door before Jessica could think of a good reply.

"Sheesh, why does it take so long for pieces to disintegrate?" Jessica said. She was standing by the sink, running cold water and the disposal as Elizabeth and Mr. Wakefield finished their breakfast.

"At least the disposal likes them," Elizabeth said with a grin as she brought her empty cereal bowl over to load into the dishwasher. Pulling open the door, she groaned. "We didn't just forget the disposal, Jess. Look at this." She stood back to reveal a dishwasher chock-full of dirty dishes.

"Ugh," Jessica said promptly. "Didn't you remember you were supposed to run it last night?"

"Me? It was your turn!"

"No, it wasn't," Jessica replied, turning to face her twin. "I did it the night before."

"The night before?" Elizabeth said in amazement. "The night before was the party. You didn't run the dishwasher then, either."

Jessica folded her arms. She knew Elizabeth was

right, but she hated to give up a good argument. "Well, neither did you," she shot back. Which was true, as far as it went.

"Girls, girls," Mr. Wakefield said over the top of his newspaper.

"I guess it doesn't matter all that much," Elizabeth said in a small voice. "If you hand me the detergent, Jess, I'll be happy to run it."

Jessica managed a smile herself and handed Elizabeth the box. "Here you, go, Elizabeth," she said sweetly as she massaged her temple. Running a household was starting to give her a headache.

"What we need is a fairy godmother," Jessica said as she and Elizabeth rode their bikes to downtown Sweet Valley an hour later. She imagined a fairy with a silver wand, making beautiful things happen to Mrs. Wolsky's sunporch.

Elizabeth gave a low laugh. "What we need are some good, cheap pieces of furniture!" she corrected her sister.

The girls came to a stop near Sweet Valley Furniture, Inc., and locked up their bikes. "Now, remember," Jessica reminded Elizabeth as they went into the building, "I'm going to do the talking, OK?" Elizabeth nodded. "Just look like you know what you're doing. That always impresses the salespeople."

The twins had been in the store a few times before but never by themselves. They roamed from one section to another, looking as though they were examining the furniture for quality and workmanship. But mostly, they were examining the price tags.

"Two hundred dollars for this?" Elizabeth whispered, looking at a small coffee table.

"It does seem a little steep," Jessica replied. "But it's got a red sticker. That means it's on sale."

"For what?" Elizabeth peered over her twin's shoulder.

"A hundred and seventy-five," Jessica read. Shuddering, she dropped the tag. "Come on, let's try the other end of the store. Maybe they've got a sale section over there."

"Do they do one-tenth price?" Elizabeth murmured, following her sister.

"What are you kids doing?" someone said behind them. Elizabeth turned to see a tall, heavyset man with gray hair blinking at them rapidly from behind a pair of thick glasses. "Are you with an adult?"

"No, sir," Elizabeth stammered.

The man frowned. "Then I'm going to have to ask you to leave."

"Excuse me, sir," Jessica piped up. Elizabeth swung around to see her sister step forward, arms folded across her chest. "We're here on an important errand. We've been sent by our mother, who's one of Sweet Valley's finest interior design artists. She's asked us to pick out some very expensive furniture for a client. And if you don't want us here, then we'll take our business someplace else." She stared hard at the gray-haired man, who blinked again.

"Very expensive furniture?" the man asked.

"*Very* expensive," Jessica repeated.

"And your mother is—?"

"Alice Wakefield," Jessica said bravely. She waited to see how the man would take this news. *I hope he doesn't try to call her at home,* she thought, crossing her fingers.

But the salesman seemed impressed. "Alice Wakefield? Very well. What did your mother have in mind?"

Jessica smiled triumphantly. "We were interested in a coffee table like the one over here," she told the man.

"That is, she was interested in it," Elizabeth put in.

"Only not quite so big and bulky," Jessica went on. "Maybe something a little smaller and—" She meant to say "cheaper" but decided not to.

"Lighter," Elizabeth said, nodding.

The salesman put his hand on his chin. "Did your mother have a preference as to type? Is it to be utilitarian, perhaps, or purely decorative?"

"Oh, purely decorative," Jessica said quickly.

"Utilitarian," Elizabeth said at the same time.

They looked at each other in confusion. "Well, both," Jessica said, and flashed the salesman her biggest smile. "If possible. As long as it's really nice and isn't too—"

"Big and bulky," Elizabeth finished.

The salesman scratched his head. "If you'll step this way, ladies," he said at last, leading them to an alcove filled with coffee tables. "This might be the sort of thing your mother is looking for." He pointed to a small brown coffee table with three legs.

"Oh!" Jessica said.

"Ah!" Elizabeth contributed. They stood there for a moment while Jessica tried to think of something to say next.

"Would you like to inspect it further?" the salesman asked.

"It looks very nice," Jessica said. "What's the cost?"

The salesman consulted a list. "About three fifty. Plus tax, of course, and shipping charges should your mother wish to have it delivered."

The girls looked at each other, hardly daring to believe their ears. Jessica found her voice first. "Three dollars and fifty cents?" she asked with excitement.

The man made a harrumphing noise deep in his throat. "Certainly not! Three hundred and fifty dollars. I believe you mentioned that your mother's client has plenty of money to spend?"

"Oh—yes, plenty." With a sinking heart, Jessica tried again. "Could you show us one of your cheapest models, just for comparison's sake?"

"Certainly. Right this way." He led them to a table that was no larger than a VCR and painted with red and white stripes. Jessica thought it was the ugliest piece of furniture she had ever seen. She ran her hand over the surface. It looked like plastic pretending to be wood, and it felt the same way.

"I see." Jessica tried to sound sophisticated. "And the price?"

The salesman consulted the tag. "Only seventy-five dollars."

Elizabeth winced.

Jessica was about to also but caught herself just in time. "I see," she said again, nodding.

"Would Mrs. Wakefield be interested in the Allingham table?" the salesman went on. Behind his glasses, his eyes were now blinking even more quickly.

"The what?" Jessica couldn't stop herself this time.

"The Allingham table. The brown one I showed you first." He pulled at his bow tie and looked impatiently at Jessica.

"Ah," Jessica said wisely. "The Allingham table. Yes. I'm afraid it just doesn't suit. Too—too—"

"Too big and bulky," Elizabeth said.

"Exactly." Jessica nodded.

The salesman shrugged and consulted his watch. "Very well," he said. "I imagine your mother has more than just a coffee table in mind?"

"Oh, definitely," Jessica assured him. "We have—that is, she has—an entire sunporch to decorate."

"Perhaps it would be better to begin with a

couch, in that case," the salesman went on. "Or perhaps I should call Mrs. Wakefield directly for any further particulars?" He stared hard at Jessica.

"Um—" Wondering how to respond, Jessica remembered a line that Steven had used that morning. "Thanks very much," she said gravely, shaking hands with the salesman. "Don't call us, we'll call you."

Mrs. Wakefield woke up early Saturday morning, just as she had on Friday. But this time, she didn't go back to sleep.

She couldn't.

I guess I'm just programmed to be an early riser, she said to herself, as the sun's rays streamed in through the window. One day of sleeping late was wonderful. Two seemed downright impossible. Still, Mrs. Wakefield waited till the house was quiet before going down to the kitchen.

Only her husband was still there, finishing up the last section of the newspaper. "Good morning, dear," he said as she slid into the seat opposite him. "You're really enjoying this being-a-kid business, I guess."

"What gives you that idea?" Mrs. Wakefield asked.

"Two days in a row you've slept late," Mr. Wakefield pointed out with a smile. "Can I get you some cereal?"

"Cereal?" Mrs. Wakefield considered the offer.

Cereal sounded good, but she was a kid, after all. "No, thanks. I'll just fix myself a sugar doughnut."

"Oh?" Mr. Wakefield raised his eyebrows.

Mrs. Wakefield got up and grabbed another doughnut from the box. It felt a little hard, and she realized with a sinking feeling that she'd forgotten to close up the box yesterday. *No, scratch that,* she told herself. She'd done it on purpose.

"Are the kids gone?" Mrs. Wakefield asked.

Mr. Wakefield nodded. "I'm not sure where they went, but don't expect them back anytime soon."

"Excellent," Mrs. Wakefield murmured. She checked the clock. *As long as they aren't back by eleven thirty,* she told herself.

"So what kind of things should we kids do today?" Mrs. Wakefield asked, taking a bite from her doughnut and carefully closing the box.

Mr. Wakefield laughed without taking his eyes off the paper. "*We* kids? I don't know about you, Alice, but I've got things to do today. The van needs servicing, and I have to get down to the hardware store before noon. And there are some papers from work I really need to go through. I'd love to play, but—" He shrugged. "Enjoy it while it lasts."

"Thanks," Mrs. Wakefield said, a note of irritation creeping into her voice. She got up to pour herself some of the lemonade Jessica had bought to go with the pizza. A good breakfast drink for a kid.

Her husband watched her. "Seriously, Alice, it's a great opportunity."

Mrs. Wakefield frowned. "I guess you're right." She took another bite of the doughnut. "What do the kids do on Saturdays, anyway?" she asked.

"Rollerblade?" Mr. Wakefield suggested.

Mrs. Wakefield shuddered. "Thanks. I don't want to think about that one just yet."

"Sometimes they watch TV," Mr. Wakefield added.

Mrs. Wakefield nodded. TV, that was right. And TV meant VCRs, which meant Elizabeth's media-class project. "Care to help me with my homework?" she asked sweetly.

Mr. Wakefield nearly choked on his coffee. "I beg your pardon?"

"I need to program the VCR," Mrs. Wakefield explained. She hoped she didn't need to go into more detail.

"VCR? No problem." Mr. Wakefield stood up from his chair and headed for the living room. "Just give me a tape." He held out his hand. Mrs. Wakefield handed him one of the blank ones she'd bought at Sweet Valley Video the day before, making sure to hide what had once been his tape of documentaries.

"Piece of cake," Mr. Wakefield announced. He tried to insert the tape. It wouldn't go in. "What's going on here?" he asked himself, pushing harder.

"Ned," Mrs. Wakefield said from over his shoulder, "you've got it backwards. Put the other side in first."

"Oh." Mr. Wakefield grinned sheepishly and turned the tape over, turning it upside down in the process.

"Ned!" Mrs. Wakefield said again. Only it was too late. With a pop the tape disappeared. A moment later, the VCR gave out six shrill beeps. The display lights faded, and the VCR went dead.

"Well, how do you like that!" Mr. Wakefield said, pressing the eject button eight times. Nothing happened.

"I don't like it at all," his wife said bitterly.

Mr. Wakefield pushed every button on the VCR he could find. Nothing worked. At last he gave the eject button three more pushes, just in case, and sat back on the couch. "I'm afraid it's broken," he said apologetically. "I'm really sorry. I guess I'll try to get it fixed."

"Today!" Mrs. Wakefield felt like crying.

"There's a place that does rush jobs like this," Mr. Wakefield went on. "It'll be a little expensive, but—"

"Right now!" Mrs. Wakefield said, clenching her teeth. Frantically unplugging wires, she pushed the whole thing into her husband's arms. A moment later, she heard the family van chugging out of the driveway.

Mrs. Wakefield collapsed into a chair. What now? she asked herself. No VCR, no media-class project. She couldn't let Elizabeth down. She couldn't let the twins win. And she still had to do the Rollerblading on Sunday.

In fact, Mrs. Wakefield told herself bitterly, the only thing she'd done to keep up her part of the bargain was the pledge form. Which she hadn't exactly done the way Jessica wanted.

Wait a minute.

The thought of the pledge form made Mrs. Wakefield remember something else. She sat perfectly still and thought back to the day before. *Where had the pledge form been?* she asked herself. Under Jessica's bed, of course. Along with dirty clothes and plenty of dust. And something else, too. *A tape!*

Mrs. Wakefield leaped up from the chair, a huge grin on her face. Jessica's *Days of Turmoil* tape! Of course! It hadn't been on the shelf with the other tapes.

Which meant it was still in Jessica's room.

Which meant, knowing how carefully Jessica did her cleaning up, that it was still under her bed.

Two minutes later, Mrs. Wakefield emerged from Jessica's room clutching the tape like a non-swimmer clutching a life preserver. She didn't even have to wait for the VCR to come back. She'd seen *Days of Turmoil* with Jessica, several times. All the episodes were exactly alike. With a huge grin, Mrs. Wakefield headed for the computer and turned it on. At least there was one machine in the house that she could operate!

Chuckling to herself, she began to type out Elizabeth's review.

*   *   *

"It's no good," Elizabeth said decisively. After their disastrous trip to the furniture store, the two girls had consoled themselves with a stop at the beach and a visit to Casey's for ice cream. Now they were on their way home. "I hate to say it, but there's just no way we can get the sunporch done."

"I guess you're right," Jessica admitted sadly, swerving her handlebars to avoid a pothole. "So what are we going to do?"

Elizabeth tilted her head slightly to glance at her sister. "We don't have much choice, do we? We're going to have to switch back and become kids again."

"What, and admit defeat?" Jessica scoffed, pedaling as hard as she could.

Elizabeth sighed. "I know, Jess. I don't like it, either. But what do you want to do? Kill Mom's career?"

"Not really," Jessica grumbled.

"Well, that's what's going to happen if Mrs. Wolsky's porch doesn't get done," Elizabeth argued. She strained to keep up with her twin. "It'll be really embarrassing to admit that we couldn't do it, but we've got to trade back again." *At least that way no one will go to the hospital from eating our cooking,* she added to herself.

Jessica glanced back around to face Elizabeth. "'Embarrassing' isn't the word," she said. "I just can't walk in there and tell Mom we couldn't do it!

Anyway, I *know* being a kid is harder than being an adult." She hunched her shoulders and pedaled even faster.

"Maybe it would be, if Mom had a different job," Elizabeth said. She followed Jessica around a corner, wishing her sister would slow down. "It's not like we lost or anything," she called to Jessica.

Jessica slowed her pace enough for Elizabeth to catch up. "What do you mean, we didn't lose?"

"Think of how much trouble Mom's been having with our jobs," Elizabeth told her. "The VCR was bad enough, and she hasn't even thought about Rollerblading yet."

Jessica gave a tight smile. "Yeah. She's not going to know what hit her when she gets up on those skates."

"Right," Elizabeth said. "I bet she'll be really happy to switch," she told Jessica, trying hard to convince herself as well. "She'll probably agree in a second." *Then we'll all hug one another and be back to normal again,* she thought longingly.

Jessica slowed the pace even more. She gave Elizabeth a sideways glance. "You think so?"

Elizabeth nodded as they turned onto their street.

"All right," Jessica agreed at last, coasting to a stop in the driveway. "But you do the talking this time, OK?"

"OK," Elizabeth said as she got off her bicycle. "Ready?" She swallowed hard.

"Ready," Jessica said without much enthusiasm. "I guess."

The twins found Mrs. Wakefield in the study, clicking away at the computer keyboard. "Hi, there!" she said cheerfully as Jessica and Elizabeth came in.

"Uh-oh," Jessica whispered to her sister. "I don't like that smile."

"Mom," Elizabeth said quickly, dismissing her sister's remark, "we don't know how to tell you this, but—well, we'd like to trade back." She took a deep breath as Mrs. Wakefield stopped typing. "We agree that being a parent is harder than we'd thought and—uh—"

"And we thought since you were having lots of trouble being a kid, you'd want to trade back, too," Jessica put in quickly. She breathed a secret sigh of relief. There. She'd said it, and it wasn't so bad after all.

Mrs. Wakefield laughed. "Trouble being a kid? Whatever gave you that idea, girls?"

Jessica's heart sank. "Well, the VCR . . ." she began.

Mrs. Wakefield chuckled again. "The VCR? Oh, I took care of that. It's easy to be a kid. You just have to figure out how to get around things, that's all." She indicated the computer screen. "I'm on page four of your media-class project already, Elizabeth. I think you'll get an *A*."

"But—how did you get it going?" Elizabeth asked.

Mrs. Wakefield shrugged. "Kids' assignments are easy, that's all. Speaking of assignments, how's Mrs. Wolsky's porch coming?"

Jessica decided not to answer the question. She also decided this was no time for pride. She hated to see her mother have such an easy time as a kid, and she wanted to put an end to it once and for all. "Could we switch back?" she asked in her best begging voice.

"Please?" Elizabeth put in.

Mrs. Wakefield looked back to the keyboard. Jessica could see her smile reflected in the screen as she shook her head.

"Sorry, girls," she said. She began clicking away again. "When you're an adult, you can't expect that people will bail you out every time something goes wrong. Now, if you'll excuse me, I have a media-class project to finish."

Nine

"This has been the worst day of my entire life," Jessica grumbled at five o'clock on Saturday afternoon.

"It's been pretty bad," Elizabeth agreed. The girls were sitting on their own sunporch, surrounded by a few last-minute sketches for Mrs. Wolsky's. Even Jessica had to admit that none of them were any good. The girls' combined life's savings might have purchased one leg of the Allingham coffee table. Mrs. Wolsky would probably want more furniture than that.

"Of course," Jessica considered, "I said that about yesterday, too."

"And the day before," Elizabeth reminded her.

Jessica sighed and crossed her legs. "Face it, Lizzie—it's been a totally miserable few days."

"And it's not over yet," Elizabeth pointed out. "We still have dinner to cook tonight. Not to mention figuring out what to do about Mrs. Wolsky's porch."

"You don't think we'll be sent to jail, do you?" Jessica asked suddenly.

"For what?"

"For not doing Mrs. Wolsky's sunporch."

A look of worry crossed Elizabeth's face, but she shook it away. "I don't think so. Remember, Mrs. Wolsky signed a contract with Mom, not with us. I guess she could have Mom arrested if it never gets done, though."

"Do you think Mom knows that?" Jessica said hopefully. "We could tell her she'll go to jail if we don't finish it. Then maybe she'll switch back again." It was worth a try, anyway.

Elizabeth smiled weakly. "I'm sure Mom knows what the laws are. Besides, they'd never put her in jail just for missing one deadline. Maybe if she wasn't finished by December or something."

"Then we're really sunk," Jessica groaned, sliding down onto the love seat and covering her eyes.

"Uh-huh." Elizabeth nodded sadly. "But I do have an idea about dinner."

"What is it?"

"We'll go down to the Dairi Burger and buy hamburgers for everybody. It'll cost a lot, but I think it'll be worth it."

Jessica uncovered her eyes and looked at

Elizabeth. "But Lizzie, Mom and Dad almost never bring home fast food. They're not going to like it."

"I know," Elizabeth agreed. "Do you have a better idea? I mean, we've already messed up everything else. I'm sure they'd rather have tasty fast-food than our own cooking again."

"True," Jessica said slowly. Then she sat bolt upright. "I've got it!" she announced. "We'll get the burgers, but we won't tell them."

"Huh?" Elizabeth asked.

"We get the burgers," Jessica went on, as the plan began to take shape. "Then we go into the kitchen and keep everybody out. We'll throw away the wrappers, and we'll cut the burgers in half so they won't look like they came from a store."

A grin began to cover Elizabeth's face. "That way they'll think we cooked it ourselves."

"It's perfect!" Jessica said. "We can load the burgers up with tomato slices. You can't get them that way at the Dairi Burger."

"And we already have three different kinds of mustard," Elizabeth added, her eyes dancing mischievously.

"OK," Jessica told her, standing up. "I'll go down to the Dairi Burger on my bike. Can I borrow your backpack? It's bigger than mine."

"Sure," Elizabeth said. "I'll close off the kitchen. Think I should put a frying pan in the sink or something?"

"That's a good idea. I think this will work,"

Jessica said, grinning at her sister. "As long as no one sees that all the hamburger patties are still in the freezer, anyway."

"I'll chase away anyone who tries to open the freezer," Elizabeth promised. "I'll threaten to hit them with a spatula."

"How about a lock and a chain and a sign that says 'Keep Out'?" Jessica suggested with a giggle. "Especially for Steven!"

"Did you get everything?" Elizabeth asked half an hour later. She was pleased that Jessica was back so soon. She'd spent the last twenty minutes banging pots and pans around, in case anyone was listening, and it was beginning to get a little boring.

Jessica flung two bags down on the table. "It wiped out most of my savings, but here it is. I got one burger for both of us, and two each for everybody else. Plus a bucket of potato salad. That should do it, don't you think?"

"Their burgers are pretty thick," Elizabeth mused, wiping her hands on the apron she'd put on in case anyone came to the kitchen door. "But I don't know about Steven. Will two be enough for him?" *Three might have made more sense*, she found herself thinking. *Maybe even four.*

"It better." Jessica frowned and began unwrapping hamburgers. "Load them up with tomatoes and cut them in half. I'll get out the mustard. How should we disguise the potato salad?" She took the top off the container and spooned the salad carefully into a bowl.

"Let's see," Elizabeth said, thinking hard. "Add some tomatoes, I guess, and some pepper. And don't forget to throw the container away."

Jessica picked up the empty bucket and tossed it into the garbage. "How much pepper?" She reached for the grinder.

"Enough to make it look different!" Elizabeth said, slicing a burger in half. She began to spread the mustard across the top. *It ought to work*, she told herself cheerfully. *See, it looks different already*.

"You know, this actually looks good," Steven said in amazement as he looked at his dinner plate that night.

"Surprise, surprise," Jessica snapped.

Mr. Wakefield looked up from his meal. "Say, these are delicious, girls. A few too many tomatoes, maybe, but that's all right. They remind me of something. But I can't think just what."

"Dairi Burgers," Steven said promptly, biting off an enormous mouthful of hamburger and washing it down with a glass of milk. Jessica looked at Elizabeth in alarm. "They're like Dairi Burgers. Not as good, though."

"Hmm." Mr. Wakefield took another bite. "You're right, Steven. They're almost as good as Dairi Burgers. Congratulations, girls."

"Thanks," Jessica said, breathing a sigh of relief.

Mrs. Wakefield served herself some potato salad. "This looks good, too," she said, smiling at the twins. "I didn't know you could make potato salad."

"Nothing to it," Jessica said modestly, thinking back. Had she remembered to throw the container away?

"What cookbook has the recipe?" Mrs. Wakefield wanted to know. "I really like all the pepper you've used."

"Oh—" Elizabeth shrugged. "Just some cookbook. I forget which one."

Mrs. Wakefield swallowed. "Maybe after dinner you'll show me. When I'm your mother again, I'd like to make it for you sometime."

"Actually, Mom," Jessica said quickly, "the recipe came from a school project. I'm afraid we don't have a copy here."

"Oh." Mrs. Wakefield's face fell. "Maybe you can write it out for me?"

Jessica smiled. "When I get a chance," she promised.

The rest of the dinner passed quickly. At last there was only half a hamburger remaining on the plate. "Mom? Dad?" Jessica said politely, offering it around.

"No, thanks, dear," Mrs. Wakefield said. "I'm full." Their father smiled and shook his head.

"You forgot me," Steven said, reaching for it.

"What have you had, six already?" Jessica

asked, passing him the plate: Steven peeled open the top of the bun. "Ugh," he said, his lip curling back in disgust.

"What's the matter?" Elizabeth asked.

"The mustard," Steven said. "Why did you have to go and put mustard on all the burgers anyway? I don't like this kind."

"Picky, picky!" Jessica teased him.

"Why don't you just scrape it off?" Elizabeth asked.

"It's not the same that way," Steven told her, a scowl on his face. "It doesn't get rid of the taste."

"Why don't you scrape it off and put on the kind of mustard you like?" his father asked. "That should disguise it all right, and I'm sure there's still plenty of mustard left in the kitchen."

"OK," Steven said. He picked up his plate and walked toward the kitchen.

Elizabeth nudged Jessica. "Did you throw everything away?" she whispered.

"Yes," Jessica whispered back, hoping that she had.

"What are you two whispering about?" Mrs. Wakefield asked.

"Never mind," they said together.

Jessica stood up. "I'll think go check on how Steven's coming along. The mustard can be kind of hard to find."

As she walked toward the kitchen, Steven came through the door, holding his hamburger plate in one hand and carrying something in the other. "Oh, Mo-om," he sang out. "You wanted to know the recipe for the potato salad?"

"Give me that!" Jessica cried, leaping out of her chair and grabbing for Steven's wrist.

"Not a chance," Steven said, holding the potato salad lid high above his head. "Here's the recipe. Step one: Go to Dairi Burger and buy a bucket of their potato salad. Step two:—"

"Give it to me!" Jessica insisted, stomping on Steven's foot.

"Ow! Step two: Add pepper and tomatoes. Step three: Serve and pretend you made it yourself." Lowering the lid, he handed it disdainfully to Jessica. "Here you go. No wonder the burgers were so good."

"Well, I still think it was worth a try," Jessica said afterward. Once again, the two girls were curled up on their sunporch.

Elizabeth played with the wicker on her chair. "I guess," she agreed. "It was better than cooking, anyway. So now all we have to do is Mrs. Wolsky's porch. Or should I say, figure out what will happen to us when we don't get it done by tomorrow evening."

"We'll probably be grounded for a year," Jessica predicted.

"Two years," Elizabeth said. "And bread and water for a month."

"At least." Jessica picked up a pillow from the couch and settled it behind her head. "No bikes, no Rollerblades, no nothing."

"I'll probably have to give up working on the newspaper," Elizabeth said gloomily.

"My social life will be completely ruined," Jessica said, stretching her legs out onto the wicker coffee table. She looked around her. "I guess I'd better memorize the rest of the house. I have a feeling we'll be spending most of our teenage years locked in our bedrooms. You know, I'll really miss this sun—" She broke off abruptly and grabbed her sister's hand. "Oh, Elizabeth, I've got the most wonderful idea!"

Elizabeth raised an eyebrow. "What is it?"

Jessica smiled proudly. "Guess!"

"I can't, Jess," Elizabeth said impatiently. "Tell me."

"It's really great!" Jessica said, looking her sister in the eye. "It's so amazing! We're not going to have to be grounded at all!"

"*What?*" Elizabeth asked again.

Jessica pulled Elizabeth toward her. "We can decorate Mrs. Wolsky's porch to look like ours," she announced triumphantly.

Elizabeth frowned. "This is a nice porch, Jess, but our furniture probably cost a lot of money, too."

"That's not what I mean, Lizzie. We can get Mrs. Wolsky's porch to look *exactly* like ours."

Elizabeth still didn't see. "How?"

"It's a good thing our porch furniture is made of

light wicker," Jessica went on, speaking slowly and distinctly. "And it's a good thing Mrs. Wolsky only lives a few houses down the street."

Elizabeth's mouth fell open as she realized at last what Jessica meant. "You wouldn't!"

"I would, too!" Jessica told her. "And so would you. Mrs. Wolsky can't complain. Mom designed this porch. All we have to do is bring the furniture down to Mrs. Wolsky's, set it up, and make sure no one comes into this room for a while."

"Hmm," Elizabeth said thoughtfully. "There's got to be a catch somewhere."

"What kind of a catch could there be?" Jessica asked.

"I don't know," Elizabeth told her. "But it seems that there's always a catch when you come up with wild ideas like this."

"Well, do you have a better idea?" Jessica demanded. "No offense or anything, but it's kind of late to be picking holes in my plans if you don't have one of your own. Or would you rather live down in the crawl space with the rats?"

Elizabeth twisted a lock of her hair. The plan seemed a little like stealing, but she had to admit, they were pretty desperate. "I think it's a great idea, Jessica," she told her sister, swallowing hard. "Let's do it!"

My last day to be a kid, Mrs. Wakefield thought when she woke up early on Sunday morning. She yawned and swung her legs over the side of the bed. With the media-class project done, there would be plenty of time today for fun things that she always seemed to be too busy to do. Bike riding, for sure. Curling up with a good book in the backyard tree—just the kind of thing Elizabeth liked best. Maybe call a few friends to chat, as Jessica would. It promised to be a fine morning. Mrs. Wakefield hummed to herself as she headed downstairs.

Then she remembered the Rollerblades.

Mrs. Wakefield squared her shoulders and took a deep breath. *If the kids can, so can I*, she told herself. She only hoped she sounded convincing.

Opening the shutters, Mrs. Wakefield heard noises on the sidewalk. Two Rollerbladers came by at what Mrs. Wakefield considered an impossible speed. As they neared, she saw they were Janet and Lila. Janet's strides were long and sweeping. While not as long, Lila's seemed even more graceful. Both girls seemed to cover about ten feet of sidewalk every second. Quickly, Mrs. Wakefield closed the shutters.

Uh-oh, she thought.

No one else was in the kitchen. She took a big bite of yet another sugar doughnut. The sweet taste filled her mouth. Mrs. Wakefield chewed and swallowed. Hmm. She went to the refrigerator and filled her glass with milk, passing over the lemonade. Much as she hated to admit it, Mrs.

Wakefield was realizing that she didn't like sugar doughnuts very much.

Jessica came down the stairs, looking refreshed. "Good morning, dear," Mrs. Wakefield said.

"Hi, Mom," Jessica said, sounding much happier than she had the night before. Mrs. Wakefield looked at her curiously. "How's your sugar doughnut? Good, huh?"

"Just fine," Mrs. Wakefield agreed. "Actually, I was thinking I might make myself an omelet this morning. For a change, if you know what I mean."

"Hmm." Jessica tried to hide a smile. "I'm sorry, Mom, I don't think that's a good idea."

"What?" Mrs. Wakefield stared at her daughter in confusion.

"I'm not sure you're old enough to prepare one properly," Jessica went on. "Kids can't be trusted to do that, after all. You said something like that once yourself."

"Oh." Mrs. Wakefield leaned against the door. She remembered that conversation, all right. About three months earlier, Jessica had tried to make an omelet and had very nearly burned the house down. Mrs. Wakefield had told the girls they were not to make omelets again.

"Well, maybe you could make me one," Mrs. Wakefield began. Then she caught herself. "Never mind. I'll just eat the rest of my sugar doughnut." She forced a smile. "Yum. Yum."

Steven came in, banging the door behind him.

"Where have you been?" Jessica asked him frostily, fixing herself a bowl of cereal.

"Out videotaping the paperboy," Steven said proudly. "Got lots of great footage, too. The best part was when the poodle down the street chased him halfway to the next town."

"It went after the wrong person," Jessica commented.

Steven was about to answer her back when Mrs. Wakefield interrupted him. "Steven, could I see you in the living room for a moment, please?"

Steven shrugged. "I guess so." He followed her into the living room. "If this has to do with the VCR, Mom—"

"It doesn't," Mrs. Wakefield cut in. "I'd like to borrow your Rollerblades."

"My Rollerblades?" Steven's eyes nearly popped out of his head.

"Your Rollerblades," Mrs. Wakefield continued. Her voice sounded firmer than she felt. "The twins' won't fit." *And I'd rather die than ask them*, she added to herself. "May I borrow them?"

"Sure," Steven said, running his hand through his hair. "But you don't even know how to use them."

"I can learn," Mrs. Wakefield said.

Steven looked at her sideways. "I don't know, Mom. Maybe I should give you a couple of lessons. It's not as easy as it looks."

It looks easy? Mrs. Wakefield wanted to say. She

cleared her throat. "That would be very nice. Thank you."

"There's just one thing." Steven looked at his mother with a devilish grin.

Mrs. Wakefield frowned. "What is it?"

"That I get to film you while you learn."

"OK, start by putting them on," Steven directed his mother in the driveway. "I'll get the camera ready."

Mrs. Wakefield shoved her feet into the shoes. It wasn't as tight a fit as she'd expected. In fact, there seemed to be quite a bit of space past her toes. Well, she'd just have to stuff paper towels in the tips before starting the Rollerblade-a-thon, that was all. She snapped her blades tightly and got to her feet.

The next thing she knew, she was lying on her back in the driveway.

"Nice one, Mom," Steven called, camera whirring. "Next time, hold on to the car while you get up."

Mrs. Wakefield gingerly pulled herself into a kneeling position. The car was several feet away. She crawled over to it and braced herself against the hood.

"Good," Steven instructed her. "Now put your feet at angles to each other and push off." He demonstrated with his own feet.

"Like this?" Mrs. Wakefield did as she was told. *Oops.* The right Rollerblade started to slide and wouldn't stop. Her knee banged into the concrete of the driveway.

"Excellent!" Steven told her. "But you forgot to stop. Like this. Watch." He put the camera down and mimed what she needed to do.

"We should have started with that," Mrs. Wakefield said, preparing to stand up again. Her knee ached already, and they'd only just begun.

"I thought you wanted to learn to Rollerblade, not learn to stop Rollerblading," Steven said, snickering and picking up the camera once more. "OK. Try it now."

The camera began to whir. Mrs. Wakefield stretched out first one blade, then the other. "Good!" Steven yelled from behind the camera. "Now, see if you can stop." Mrs. Wakefield obeyed, but too quickly. This time she wound up facedown. "Ouch."

Steven came closer. "You're OK, Mom." He stuck the camera next to her face and continued to film. "It just takes time, that's all. I should have told you not to put on the brakes too quickly."

"You're not a very good teacher," Mrs. Wakefield said, getting up onto her knees again. She checked her hand, which was badly scraped.

"Well, you're not a very good student," Steven replied.

Half an hour later, Steven put his camera down. "Maybe we should call it a day," he said.

"Maybe we should," Mrs. Wakefield agreed, gasping for breath. Her right ankle throbbed. As for her knees, she was positive they had swelled to twice their normal size.

"You look kind of sick," Steven told her, extending his arm.

"Thanks a lot," his mother replied, grabbing hold of him and letting him steer her over to the steps. "This sport is a killer, Steven."

"Oh, it's not that bad," Steven told her with a grin. "You just have to get used to it. Another couple of weeks of lessons from a master teacher like me, and you'll be zipping all over town." He snapped his fingers. "Nothing to it."

"A couple of weeks?" Mrs. Wakefield cried out.

Steven looked at her carefully. "In your case, maybe a month. Don't take this personally, but you're kind of a slow learner."

Mrs. Wakefield started to unsnap the Rollerblades. *A month!* she thought angrily. *The Rollerblade-a-thon is today.* She checked her body for bruises. There were at least a dozen—to say nothing of cuts on her knees, scrapes on her hand and elbow, and a couple of sore fingers.

"Don't worry, you'll get the hang of it eventually," Steven said consolingly. Then he began to chuckle. "I can't wait to see this movie. The shot of you draped across the hood of the car! The time you went screaming across the lawn on one foot!" He laughed loudly. "It's going to be hilarious."

"Hilarious," Mrs. Wakefield echoed, wondering if you could smash a video camera with a Roller-blade.

Mrs. Wakefield staggered into the living room. *The girls will be happy to switch back*, she told herself. *It's not like I lost or something. It'll be a draw.*

"Well, you win, girls," Mrs. Wakefield said, wincing with pain as she sat down heavily on the couch. "Let's call it off."

"Call it off?" Jessica exclaimed, frowning in be-wilderment.

"That's right," Mrs. Wakefield told her. "You said you wanted to switch back. So do I. The deal's off."

"Oh, but you can't do that," Elizabeth said.

"Why not?" Mrs. Wakefield looked indignantly up at her daughters.

"That was then," Jessica said, winking at her sis-ter. "This is now."

Mrs. Wakefield looked searchingly from one twin to the other. "I'm giving up," she said impa-tiently, swallowing hard. "Don't you understand? You two were right. Being a kid is harder than I thought." *At least, Rollerblading is harder than I thought*, she added to herself. "Since you've been having trouble being adults, I thought we could just switch back."

"Trouble?" Jessica said innocently. "Are we hav-ing trouble, Lizzie?"

"I don't think so," Elizabeth answered. "It's easy being an adult. You just have to think about things, that's all."

Mrs. Wakefield widened her eyes. "You finished Mrs. Wolsky's porch?" she demanded. "How in the world did you do it so quickly?"

"A piece of cake." Jessica snapped her fingers. "Adults' assignments are easy, that's all. Are you saying you're having trouble with the Rollerblade-a-thon?"

Mrs. Wakefield frowned. "I'm begging you girls. Could we please switch back?"

Jessica solemnly shook her head. So did Elizabeth.

"Sorry, Mom," Elizabeth said. "Kids can't expect other people to keep bailing them out every time something goes wrong." She seemed to be having trouble keeping a straight face, and Mrs. Wakefield realized she'd heard that line somewhere before.

"All right," she said, struggling to her feet. "But if I die this afternoon, girls, you'll be responsible."

Ten

At two o'clock in the afternoon, Mrs. Wakefield threw the hated Rollerblades into the car and eased her bruised body into the driver's seat. "Take good care of each other," she told the girls. "I'll probably never see you again."

"Oh, Mom," Jessica said, rolling her eyes. *Really,* she told herself, *how overdramatic can you get?*

"You'll be all right," Elizabeth assured her. "You've made a lot of progress."

Mrs. Wakefield attached her seat belt and looked up at the twins. "Plenty of progress," she said with a halfhearted smile. "Now I can actually stand up on Rollerblades for thirty seconds without falling over."

"Didn't you make it to the end of the driveway a couple of times?" Elizabeth asked.

"I made it to the end of the driveway lots of

times," Mrs. Wakefield corrected her. "Unfortunately, I wasn't usually standing up when I got there. Don't forget to water the plants, and take some cooking lessons if I don't come back."

"Dad's in his study, so he won't notice as long as we're quiet," Jessica told Elizabeth on the sunporch. "Let's start with the couch—it's the biggest. You take that end." Jessica lifted up a corner of the couch. "Light as a feather," she said, letting it drop again. "Ready?"

Elizabeth got a good grip. "Uh-huh."

"OK, heave."

The girls picked up the couch easily enough. Getting it out the porch door and into the driveway was a little trickier.

"Turn it back toward me," Jessica was suggesting, when she heard a noise. Coming into the driveway was the last person she wanted to see at that moment: her brother.

"Taking the couch for a walk?" he said.

"Very funny," Jessica told him, pushing it the rest of the way through the door.

"So what are you doing with it?" Steven wanted to know.

"Nothing that concerns you," Jessica said.

"So you can go away now," Elizabeth added, starting toward the sidewalk.

Steven blocked her path. "Where are you taking this thing?" he demanded.

"None of your business," Elizabeth said firmly.

"It's not like you use any of the porch furniture," Jessica added. "When was the last time you sat out there—nineteen twenty-six?"

Steven folded his arms. "So you're getting rid of all the porch furniture, huh? Does Dad know about this?"

Jessica sighed. There didn't seem to be any way around it. She put down her end of the couch, and quickly she explained the problem of Mrs. Wolsky's sunporch. "Mrs. Wolsky can't come home to an empty house this afternoon," she finished. "We've got to get the furniture in there before it's too late."

Steven shook his head. "Mom and Dad are going to find out, you know. And then what will you do?"

"We'll think of something," Jessica assured him, waving her hand dismissively. "All we need is to get the furniture in, and everything will be OK. Don't tell, please!"

"All right," Steven said slowly. "On one condition."

"I knew it!" Elizabeth exclaimed.

"I want to film this," Steven said, rubbing his hands together. "We'll make it look like a robbery in progress. You guys will need costumes—something dark and mysterious like a cape, maybe, or a cardboard mask."

"Steven!" Elizabeth wailed.

"If you wear a paper mustache, Elizabeth, you

won't be recognized," Steven told her, his voice growing more excited. "Walk slowly, like you're real robbers, and talk only in whispers."

Jessica swallowed hard. "OK—we'll do it."

"Jess!"

"Listen, Lizzie," Jessica said, facing her sister, "what choice do we have? If we can just get the furniture into Mrs. Wolsky's house, Mrs. Wolsky will be happy—and if she's happy, Mom will be happy, right? So what's some missing porch furniture?"

"Dad's in his study," Steven said, grinning and pointing.

Elizabeth looked at the ground and sighed. "Oh, all right," she agreed. "But Steven, I just want you to know that you're a total toad."

"Thank you, ma'am," Steven said, giving her an exaggerated bow.

"This is totally embarrassing," Elizabeth said fifteen minutes later as she hefted her end of the couch. She was wearing a hooded sweatshirt that nearly covered her face, along with a ski cap she'd found at the back of the closet. Jessica had put on a black cape and a dark-blue beret. For good measure, she had drawn in a mustache and beard with eyebrow pencil.

"Don't worry, no one will know who you are in that getup," Jessica assured her as they started down the block.

"Less talking!" Steven interrupted them. "We're ready to roll!"

As the girls walked furtively along the street toward Mrs. Wolsky's house, Jessica discovered that she was enjoying herself. She slowed down her steps, walking with an exaggerated side-to-side motion. Every few seconds, she looked over her shoulder. "Hey, youse guys," she said out of one side of her mouth, the way she'd seen a gangster talk in an old black-and-white movie once. "Move dose legs!"

"What?" Elizabeth stared at her blankly.

"Cheezit! Da cops!" Jessica added. "Come on, Lizzie, get into it!"

Elizabeth only sighed.

Transferring the furniture took four trips all together. By the third time down the block, Jessica was having a blast. Walking into Mrs. Wolsky's porch with the last framed picture, she whispered to her sister: "Don't forget to grab da loot." She pronounced it to rhyme with "put."

"You mean the *loot*," Elizabeth said, rhyming it with "boot."

"Oh, excuse me," Jessica said indignantly. "Sorry, but I never been to college or nothing."

"Or *anything*," Elizabeth corrected her again.

Jessica fixed her with a look. "Elizabeth," she told her sister, "you don't know nothing."

"Take!" Steven announced, lowering his camera.

"There you are," Mr. Wakefield said to Elizabeth when she and Jessica returned from Mrs. Wolsky's.

Jessica was upstairs scrubbing off her mustache and beard, and Elizabeth had just pulled off her costume. "Is Jessica with you?"

Elizabeth nodded.

"Thank goodness," Mr. Wakefield said, sounding relieved. "I just had this peculiar phone call from Mr. Jantzen across the street. He told me this long story about thieves and burglars skulking around our property."

"Really?" Elizabeth said, a touch of red creeping into her cheeks.

"That's what he said," Mr. Wakefield replied. "He said he saw two of them. They were small, he said, and one of them was completely covered up, but the other one had a beard and mustache. I'm glad you're safe. Have you seen anything mysterious?"

Jessica came out of the bathroom, her chin glistening but clean. "Mysterious like what?"

"No, we haven't seen anything mysterious at all," Elizabeth said hastily, darting her twin a look. "But maybe we should search the house just in case. We'll take the downstairs, and you can have the upstairs."

"That's too much for you two," he father said, shaking his head. "Suppose I do the porch and the patio, too?"

"Oh, we'll take care of the porch," Elizabeth said quickly. "Why don't you search the kitchen instead?"

*　　*　　*

"Nothing mysterious on the porch, Dad," Elizabeth said as the girls joined their father in the living room.

"What about you?" Jessica asked. "Find any desperadoes?"

"No desperadoes," he said, looking thoughtfully at a large object in his hands, "but I did find this on top of the refrigerator. I think it's supposed to be for you."

Elizabeth took the framed collage he held out to them. Across the top, "Why I'm the luckiest mother in the world" was written in beautiful calligraphy.

"It's from Mom," Elizabeth said slowly, recognizing the handwriting. Her eyes flicked across the collage. It was covered with pictures of Mrs. Wakefield and the twins. The girls as babies, smiling up at the camera. The girls as toddlers, exploring the playground. The girls dressed for their first day of kindergarten, Mrs. Wakefield proudly holding each one by the hand. Elizabeth recognized more recent pictures, too—even an occasional picture of Steven.

"It's beautiful," Elizabeth murmured. "She even put pressed flowers between the pictures. They're from the backyard, aren't they?"

"Oh, Lizzie, listen to this! 'A daughter's a daughter all of her life,'" Jessica read from a caption near one of the photographs. Her eyes misted. "I can't believe she did this for us."

"How about this one?" Elizabeth said. "'J is for

the Joy that's in your smile; E for the Excitement that you share; S, your Sunshine warms me all the while'— Jess, look!" she exclaimed. "This is for you. It spells out 'Jessica.'"

"And here's another poem that spells your name," Jessica pointed out. "This is gorgeous."

Elizabeth blinked back tears. "Why didn't she show it to us before?" she asked aloud. "Why did she hide it on top of the refrigerator?"

Mr. Wakefield spoke up. "I think she was planning to give it to you the night of the mother-daughter party," he said, "but—" He spread out his arms and shrugged.

The girls looked at each other. "Are you thinking what I'm thinking, Elizabeth?" Jessica asked.

Elizabeth nodded. "Let's go!"

Jessica led the way to the Rollerblade-a-thon course. The twins brought their bikes to a stop close to the finish line, and watched the Boosters as they came nearer. Janet Howell was in front. She was surrounded by kids on bicycles, urging her on. Just behind her, Amy Sutton's blades churned frantically. Janet and Amy flashed past. One by one the other contestants did the same. Except one.

"Where's Mom?" Jessica said, looking down at the empty course.

"We'd better go find her," Elizabeth said with a frown. "Let's ride back along the loop till we get to her."

"Good idea." The girls mounted their bikes and headed back along the course. Besides an occasional pedestrian or dog, no one was in sight.

"Do you think she's hurt?" Elizabeth bit her lip.

Jessica threw her bicycle into a higher gear. "If anything happens to Mom, I'll probably never forgive myself," she said, pedaling harder. "I should have known better than to send her out with Rollerblades on."

"We should have switched back," Elizabeth agreed.

"We were incredibly selfish," Jessica said. She looked over her shoulder. "Where *is* she?" The girls were more than halfway around the course, and their mother was nowhere in sight.

About two miles from the finish line, Jessica abruptly put on the brakes. "That's her," she whispered, half to herself.

The girls pulled their bikes to a stop and stared. It was their mother, all right—but it was hard to tell. She was puffing and looked drenched with sweat. Her Rollerblades were sliding all over the road—Jessica guessed she was going just as far side to side as forward. Her pants were ripped at the knee.

"She can't even stand up straight," Jessica said softly. "Look at her, Lizzie. It's so hard for her, and I didn't even help her when she needed it—I only laughed!"

"I know," Elizabeth whispered. "So did I."

It's my project, and she did it for me, Jessica thought. *No matter how hard it was, she didn't give up!* She felt a surge of love and admiration as she watched. "She's doing it, Lizzie. She's going to finish the course, I know she is!"

"Yes," Elizabeth said softly, not taking her eyes off Mrs. Wakefield. "She isn't going to let us down."

"Let's cheer for her," Jessica suggested suddenly. "We can ride with her all the rest of the way."

But Elizabeth shook her head. "Come on," she hissed to her twin. "Let's go the other way—it's the quickest way back to the finish line."

"What are you—?"

"We need to get there before everyone goes home," Elizabeth explained.

"I still don't—" Jessica began, but Elizabeth was already speeding away.

Eleven

"Listen, you guys," Elizabeth said as she and Jessica crossed the finish line, where the Boosters were all standing. "Jessica and I really want to apologize for Thursday night. We want to make it up to you."

"We do?" Jessica said, staring hard at her sister. "When?"

Elizabeth was so proud of her plan, she couldn't keep from grinning. "Tonight!" she said. Then she turned to Amy. "But I'll need a little help.

In the gathering twilight, Mrs. Wakefield Rollerbladed on toward the finish line. A final stride, and she was over the finish line at last.

"Congratulations!" Amy said, as Mrs. Wakefield sank to the ground in exhaustion.

"Thank you, Amy," Mrs. Wakefield said, panting. "Where's everyone else?"

"Oh, they've gone," Amy said promptly. "You were a little later than everyone expected—I mean—" She clapped her hand to her mouth in dismay.

"Never mind, Amy," Mrs. Wakefield said with a wan smile. "I know what you mean." Still in a sitting position, she started to loosen the snaps on the Rollerblades. "I will never do this again as long as I live."

"Oh, it's not so bad, Mrs. Wakefield," Amy said with a little laugh. "It's easier than—"

"Than it looks." Mrs. Wakefield finished the sentence for her and looked murderously at Steven's Rollerblades. "Yes, Amy, I think I've heard that somewhere before. Listen, I appreciate your waiting for me."

"No problem," Amy assured her. "I wonder if you could give me a ride to your house. Elizabeth and I have to work on our media-class project."

"But Elizabeth's is done," Mrs. Wakefield said with surprise.

"Oh." Amy looked puzzled. "Well, what I meant to say was that mine isn't, and she said she'd give me a few tips."

"OK." Mrs. Wakefield was too tired to press the point. She slipped her own shoes on and threw the Rollerblades into the back of the car with as much force as she could muster.

*   *   *

"That's strange," Mrs. Wakefield said as she pulled into the driveway. The house was completely dark. "I can't imagine where Elizabeth's gotten to."

"She said she would be here," Amy insisted. She opened the passenger door and got out.

Mrs. Wakefield climbed out of the car, too, wincing with pain. She slammed the car door shut. As she did, lights popped on all over the house! *How peculiar,* Mrs. Wakefield said to herself. Then, as if in a daze, she saw her entire family come running out the front door.

"Surprise!" they were shouting.

Mrs. Wakefield stared, her sore legs almost giving way. "What's going on?" she gasped.

"Happy Mother's Day!" Jessica and Elizabeth shouted at once.

"It was Lizzie's idea, Mom," Jessica told Mrs. Wakefield a few minutes later. "We loved the collage you made for us, so we decided to do something wonderful for you, too." She gently helped her mother into the most comfortable chair in the living room and winked across at her sister.

"We realized we don't always appreciate what you do for us," Elizabeth continued, bringing an ice pack for Mrs. Wakefield's biggest bruise.

"And it's hard work being an adult," Jessica added. "We know that by now!"

Mrs. Wakefield looked as if she was about to cry.

"This is wonderful, girls," she told them, giving them each a big hug. "But what's that noise coming from the backyard?"

Jessica smiled across at her twin. "It was your idea, so you should tell her," she said.

Elizabeth's eyes sparkled. "Since we messed up Thursday's party, we thought we'd do it all over again—but this time we'd do it right."

"All our guests are out back!" Jessica jumped in.

"They are?" Mrs. Wakefield exclaimed.

"Having a great time," Jessica added. "I remembered the charcoal."

"And I brought the chips and the napkins," Elizabeth said proudly. "Steven even bought a bottle of pop—if you can believe it."

"And the rest of his tomatoes," Jessica said with a giggle.

"And I drove them home in the van, along with all those groceries," Mr. Wakefield said. "Don't I deserve some credit, too?"

"You all deserve credit," Mrs. Wakefield said, her eyes shining. "This is glorious. This is—" Stopping in the middle of the sentence, Mrs. Wakefield shook her head and took a deep breath. "I'm so proud and happy to be your mother," she said, hugging them one more time. "And guess what I realized?"

"What?" Jessica asked.

"That it's harder to be a kid than an adult," Mrs. Wakefield admitted.

* * *

"I wanted to tell you personally," Ellen Riteman said, walking into the living room, where Mrs. Wakefield was talking with Mrs. Sutton about the Rollerblade-a-thon. "This lemonade is excellent—and just enough ice, too."

Mrs. Wakefield smiled at her from her easy chair. She had decided that the chairs out on the patio weren't quite comfortable enough, but mothers and kids kept coming into the living room to say hello.

"I'm amazed you had the time," Mrs. Sutton said when Ellen left. "It seems to me you were terribly busy with a decorating project, weren't you?"

Mrs. Wakefield shifted her weight in the chair. "As a matter of fact . . ." she began, when the telephone rang.

Jessica bounded into the room and scooped up the receiver. "Hello?" she said. Then she held her hand over the mouthpiece. "Mom!" she stage-whispered. "It's for you." She brought the receiver over to Mrs. Wakefield's chair and rushed back out of the room.

"Thank you, dear," Mrs. Wakefield said. "Alice Wakefield," she said into the receiver.

"Mrs. Wakefield." The voice sounded vaguely familiar.

"Yes?"

There was a sniff from the other end of the line. "I don't know how you've done it, Mrs. Wakefield, but I must say I'm tremendously impressed by the job you've done on my sunporch. *Tremendously* impressed. I intend to recommend you to all my friends."

Mrs. Wakefield took the receiver off her head and stared at it. Mrs. Wolsky! No wonder she hadn't quite recognized the voice. When had she heard Mrs. Wolsky sounding happy?

Carefully Mrs. Wakefield put the receiver back against her ear. "Are you there, Mrs. Wakefield?" the voice demanded.

"I certainly am, Mrs. Wolsky," Mrs. Wakefield said, finding her tongue at last. "I'm delighted that you approve."

Sniff, sniff. "I had doubted your ability, but I shall do so no longer," Mrs. Wolsky went on. "I'm pleased to know that there is still someone on this earth who understands the greatest virtue of all."

"And which one is that, Mrs. Wolsky?" Mrs. Wakefield asked.

"Why, responsibility, of course," Mrs. Wolsky sniffed.

"We did it!" Elizabeth exclaimed to Jessica when the last guests had gone. "We were a hit!"

"You bet!" Then Jessica's face fell. "Of course, we've still got tons of cleaning up to do," she grumbled.

"Leave that to me," Mrs. Wakefield told her. "I didn't do my part on Thursday, and I didn't do anything for the party today. And since Mrs. Wolsky likes her porch, I can afford to take a couple of days off." Standing up too suddenly, Mrs. Wakefield winced. "I'll need them, too."

"That was Mrs. Wolsky?" Jessica said, arching her eyebrows. "I didn't recognize her voice."

"She likes it?" Elizabeth asked.

"She loves it," her mother corrected her. "How in the world did you do it, girls?"

Jessica and Elizabeth exchanged glances. "That's our secret," Jessica said at last. "Maybe we'll tell you tomorrow."

Twelve

◇

"I still think it's funny the way Mom got those pledges," Jessica told her sister on Monday evening. Dinner was over, and the girls had just finished Rollerblading around the block. She grinned and shook her head. "Pretty sneaky!"

Elizabeth laughed. "Well, we were pretty sneaky ourselves, bringing the porch furniture down to Mrs. Wolsky's house! But I feel better now that we've talked to Mom about it, don't you?"

"That's for sure!" Jessica declared, thinking back to dinnertime. When they'd told their mother the whole story, Mrs. Wakefield hadn't been angry at all. Instead, she'd laughed and told them how she'd collected the pledges for the Rollerblade-a-Thon.

Elizabeth took off her Rollerblades and headed

for the porch door. "That was fun, Jess. Maybe next time we can get Mom to join us."

"Maybe next year," Jessica said with a smile. Taking two more steps forward, she nearly ran into Elizabeth. "Hey, Lizzie!" she began. "What's— Hey, what's all that furniture doing here?"

The sunporch sparkled in the evening sunlight. Glancing around the room, Jessica saw a new couch, two matching chairs, a footstool, and a coffee table nicer than anything she'd seen at Sweet Valley Furniture. On the wall behind the couch hung the collage Mrs. Wakefield had given the twins for Mother's Day. *This room is so much prettier than it used to be*, Jessica thought.

"It's beautiful," Elizabeth whispered.

"Mom!" Jessica shouted, turning and darting into the living room. "Mom!" She skidded to a stop right next to the couch where her parents were sitting.

"So you've seen the porch," Mrs. Wakefield said with a chuckle, putting down the book she was reading. "Do you like it?"

"We *love* it!" Jessica corrected her, throwing her arms around her mother's neck. "But how—" she began, just as Elizabeth started to say, "But when—"

Mrs. Wakefield smiled. The corners of her eyes crinkled up. "I'm glad you like it—it was my backup plan."

"Your backup plan?" Jessica repeated, looking from her mother to her father.

"It was the final design I planned for Mrs.

Wolsky's porch," Mrs. Wakefield explained. ",
never got around to showing it to her, because you
two took over the job instead."

"So the furniture that's on our sunporch right
now was meant for Mrs. Wolsky?" Jessica asked in-
credulously.

Her mother gazed at her fondly. "It's not that I
didn't trust you two," she said, "but I couldn't risk
having you ruin my business."

"Thanks a lot!" Jessica said.

"Your mother's right," Mr. Wakefield said. "You
made Mrs. Wolsky very happy, but what if she
hadn't liked wicker furniture at all? Or what if you
hadn't come through in time for her deadline?"

Elizabeth nodded. "We thought about that," she
said.

"I'm glad," Mrs. Wakefield said. "I wanted you
to work hard, and—I'll admit it—I wanted it to be
difficult. That's the way the adult world is. But I
didn't want to destroy my reputation, either."

"That makes sense," Jessica agreed, listening in-
tently.

"So I bought the furniture on Friday afternoon,"
Mrs. Wakefield continued, "and on Saturday morning I had it delivered to the garage, so you
wouldn't see it. I figured that if you couldn't man-
age, I'd just have that furniture moved in on
Sunday." Shifting her position a little too quickly,
she winced. "But you managed. And even though
Mrs. Wolsky doesn't need that furniture, we do!"

* * *

"OK, Mom, it's time for your annual Mother's Day present!" Steven strode into the living room, a videocasette in his hand.

"I can hardly wait," Mrs. Wakefield said, settling back into her seat.

"Oh, Steven," Elizabeth said, sitting down on the couch next to her parents, "you aren't really going to—"

"Of course I am," Steven said proudly, popping a tape into the VCR.

"Oh, dear." Mrs. Wakefield sighed. On the screen, she was arguing with the twins about the Mother's Day picnic.

Mrs. Wakefield began to chuckle. "What a completely silly argument," she said, shaking her head. "What a family. Being stubborn is a family trait, all right!"

"I guess so," Jessica admitted. The next scene caught her attention. "What are you doing, Mom?"

Mrs. Wakefield gasped as she looked at the screen. Then she picked up a pillow and threw it at Steven. "Steven Wakefield!" she said. "Were you really following me around while I went and got my pledges?"

"Uh-huh," Steven said with satisfaction.

Jessica giggled and shook her head. "No wonder you couldn't get any pledges," she said with a smile, watching her mother trying to convince the neighbors to sponsor her. "You need to take some lessons!"

"It's hard being a kid," Mrs. Wakefield pointed

out, grinning sheepishly as the next scene came on the screen: two mysteriously disguised strangers stealing the porch furniture.

"Well, how do you like that—thieves!" Mr. Wakefield exclaimed, the light dawning on his face.

Elizabeth and Jessica looked at each other and giggled. "It's hard being a grown-up!" Jessica announced.

"Boo!"

Jessica looked up from her fashion magazine to see Steven bounding into the TV room. Something that looked like a stuffed stocking was draped around his neck.

Jessica turned back to her magazine, which she had opened to a section picturing short jumpers. "Is that some new kind of video camera or something? Because if it is, I'm not interested in being in any more movies."

"This is my pet boa constrictor, Eeyore," Steven explained. "You're not afraid of snakes, are you?" He held the foot of the stocking an inch from Jessica's face.

Jessica wrinkled her nose. "Excuse me, but I'm trying to read. Why don't you go play with your pet stocking or snake or whatever it is somewhere else?"

Steven flopped down on the couch. "Sheesh, what kind of a girl are you? Aren't all girls supposed to be afraid of snakes?"

Jessica gave him a sideways look. "For one thing, that isn't a snake. And for another, it takes a lot more than a stocking to scare me, or any girl for that matter. Now *boys* on the other hand . . ."

Who scares more easily, boys or girls? Find out in Sweet Valley Twins 88, STEVEN GETS EVEN.

We hope you enjoyed reading this book. If you would like to receive further information about available titles in the Bantam series, just write to the following address, with your name and address:

Kim Prior
Bantam Books
61–63 Uxbridge Road
Ealing
London W5 5SA.

If you live in Australia or New Zealand and would like more information about the series, please write to:

Sally Porter
Transworld Publishers
(Australia) Pty Ltd
15–25 Helles Avenue
Moorebank
NSW 2170
AUSTRALIA

Kiri Martin
Transworld Publishers (NZ) Ltd
3 William Pickering Drive
Albany
Auckland
NEW ZEALAND

Hang out with the coolest kids around!

THE UNICORN CLUB

Jessica and Elizabeth Wakefield are just two of the terrific members of The Unicorn Club you've met in *Sweet Valley Twins* books. Now get to know some of their friends even better!

A sensational new *Sweet Valley* series, coming soon from Bantam Books:

1. SAVE THE UNICORNS
2. MARIA'S MOVIE COMEBACK
3. THE BEST FRIEND GAME
4. LILA'S LITTLE SISTER
5. UNICORNS IN LOVE
Super Edition: UNICORNS AT WAR